A DREAMED LIFE

Sun Axelsson

A DREAMED LIFE

Translated
by
Ulla Printz-Påhlson

Ohio University Press
Athens, Ohio
London

Library of Congress Cataloging in Publication Data

Axelsson, Sun, 1935–
  A dreamed life.

  Translation of: Drömmen om ett liv.
  1. Axelsson, Sun, 1935– —Biography. 2. Authors,
Swedish—20th century—Biography. 1. Title.
PT9876.1.X45Z46413 1983   839.7'374   83-2-
196
ISBN 0–8214–0710–4
ISBN 0–8214–0711–2 (pbk.)

Revolution rages too in the
tierra caliente of each human soul.

Malcolm Lowry

It often happens, as I am sure it has happened to you. You are climbing a cliff or a diving board, your mind made up to dive into the water elegantly, head first and body gracefully poised. But up there on the platform, you look down towards the surface. It is further away than you thought. It seems impossible. Now there is a way out, that is, if you are not ashamed to admit fear: to jump in feet first. It might be a compromise, but you go through with it and you reach the depths, well and truly.

I am standing on a high cliff, the sea shimmering far below me. I am the sort of person who cannot withdraw, not even if I wanted to and could bring myself to conquer my sense of fear. There will just not be enough time before my life ends. That is why I am jumping straight back into my past, feet first into an ocean of pain and the dark abysses of my memories.

I am going to tell the story of my life.

It is difficult to talk about oneself, after having always been told that the usage of "I" and "myself" is a sign of bad manners. One should not talk about oneself. It is not nice. When I was a child I was always told that my wishes "grew in the forest on a branch." I was told that it was a bad habit to look at myself in the mirror, and "speech is silvern but silence is golden." I was a rather silent child. I was also told to strive for God's heaven, because if I did, everything else would be mine. I have been waiting for my reward close on forty years, striving for heaven by various desperate or round-about routes.

As a socialist I have always stubbornly denied the importance of myself and my own life, because all that seemed to lack importance compared to all the suffering in the world around me. I even went so far as to punish myself and others for egocentricity, vanity and shallowness. But then something strange and rather ugly kept coming to the surface from within myself.

The thing struggling to get out had been hidden for a long time, just as one can find sometimes, in some small Italian village, a mad woman kept chained in a cellar by mean relatives for fifty years on a diet of bread and water.

A part of me had been kept deep down in chains and that part started screaming and hitting out.

A slow murder was being committed, by degrees, and it was impossible to hide any longer. I had to let her out, the madwoman, who was at first unable to see or speak and whose smell was so abhorrent that I had to keep her in solitary confinement at first.

She has recently taken her first steps. She has also learned to speak after enormous difficulties—I compare her situation to Caspar Hauser's.

It has occurred to me that to get to know her might be worthwhile, for myself and for others.

Part One

For as as early as I remember I never took my self to *be* what people called me. That at least has remained crystal clear to me. That is, whatever, whoever I may be is not to be confused with the names people give *to* me, or how they *describe* me, or what they *call* me. I am not my name.

Who or what I am, as far as they are concerned is not necessarily, or thereby, *me*, as far as I am concerned.

I am presumably *what* they are describing, but not their description. I am the territory, what they say I am is their map of me.

And what I call myself to myself is, presumably, my map of me. What, o where, is the territory?

R. D. Laing

The month is August and the sun shines every day. I have found refuge in peaceful "Victoria." Victoria is an old schoolhouse, painted red, and located in a deep forest on the border between Sörmland and Västmanland.

I have withdrawn from the world to be able to write this book. It gives me a feeling of anonymity to be in this immense forest, where nature is so overwhelming that it obliterates all traces of urban anxiety, of duties and demands from society, of my abstract father, the remorseless Machine.

I really want to write this book day by day, trying to reach both the past and present but I will try and keep an open mind to whatever twists and turns the narrative will take. I am both the worker and the tool.

For a long time I had forgotten everything. I would remember small fragments of the past and with the help of make-believe I made those fragments fit the picture of my current reality or unreality. And everything would fit beautifully—however contradictory.

By and by my memory returned. Dreams helped me remember. I hunted the past until it let itself be captured and my reality in all its disintegration started to take on a definite outline.

I do not want to write a confession. I want to make my past real, to give my life substance. I want to see my experiences—that I never could take seriously or honestly believe actually had happened—take shape and form, I want my life to acquire body and soul. Today's experiences change constantly. The past that I am conjuring up is also constantly changing its meaning and content. The memories fight one another to be noticed or occasionally try to be as unobtrusive as possible.

One day they are small and ashamed and the next morning they are clamoring to be noticed, just as rowdy pupils normally at the back of the classroom sometimes surprise you by sitting in the front row.

I cannot any longer evade a thorough confrontation with the past, although a descent into the hell of the past is a painful process. It cannot be compared to Dante's Inferno, where the souls of others are tormented. In this hell I myself am tormented and punished not so much for my own ill-deeds as for others'!

The idea of writing about this confrontation only occurred to me recently. Writing about oneself is taboo for a true socialist and besides, I already had written an autobiographical novel about a little girl discreetly called Heide.

Through writing this novel, *Väktare*, I had tried to understand what caused my fear, uncertainty and anxiety during childhood and adolescence.

Väktare was written in the romantic manner. I was influenced by books on destruction and downfall, and I amused myself by alternatively letting Heide reach for the sun or look, without any illusions, into the black night where I myself dwelled. The book did not give a true picture of my life but told of an unreal and dreamlike existence.

Must one always return to the scene of the crime? Or is it possible to be liberated from childhood's clawlike fears, which act as brakes and stop one's development into maturity, with the help of the bright light of two beacons: growing older and gaining experience. Every time the light sweeps across the surface, it reveals something that was hidden and unknown, a strange reef or a newborn volcano rising from the dark.

I am no longer trying to force all things to correspond, because, depending on where I myself stand at any given moment, everything or nothing can be made to fit. I want to live in the chaos I am used to but I want to claim my boundaries, like a shelter built against harsh weather on a deserted heath.

I have already knocked down many of my own shelters and I have often been exposed to the elements while I lived in barren and desolate countries. Now, at last, I am beginning to find a small, habitable space. A small home base in the Universe.

Victoria's surroundings remind me of Slottsskogen, the expanse of parkland where I grew up. From my bedroom window I have a clear view for many kilometers across the meadows, and it gives me a feeling of endlessness and confinement, the same feeling I recognize from my childhood.

Far away, on the horizon, is the main road to Arboga and on my childhood's horizon was the road to downtown Göteborg. But it was possible to imagine,and I often did, that nothing changed, away in the distance: that Nature just went on and on, growing up into the sky with its roots firmly in the ground.

I experienced two extremes: one that my life was spent in an enclosed space with its minutes, days and years, making me feel its limitations and transience; the other that it opened up into the limitless, and further into eternity and timelessness.

Both these states of mind created anxiety in me: feelings of claustrophobia or fear of the vast expanse of eternity.

I grew up in the thirties in what was at the time a large green park, called Slottsskogen. I can only remember one kind of season, summer. My whole life was so utterly enclosed in this forest that the only way I can describe its nearness is by creating a distance.

I drew nourishment from the verdure in the same way I had sucked my mother's breast, and I felt myself growing inseparable from trees and roots, leaves and grass.

I was the youngest of four children, and the park became a second mother to me. Silently or softly whispering she received me, never tired and always without sharp edges and sounds. I left one cradle for another.

My childhood home was the official residence of the city garden architect, situated in the middle of Slottsskogen. Travelling from "Linné platsen," one had to pass two small ponds, Big and Little Pond. After that came a long and arduous uphill trek past the Seal Pond and the chance of a breather at the crest. From the crest of the hill one could see a tall house through the foliage. My childhood home. Opposite was the Swan Pond where the swans were housed through the winter months. I use the word "housed" because, according to custom, the swans had been given a large wooden house, resembling ours. Their house sat in a concrete pond, where the swans disconsolately circled, feasting on cabbage, while they shrieked and longed for the south during the dark and cold winters of the early forties.

The swans moved down to Big and Little Pond in May, and like travelling actors who have been forced to play to small and unappreciative audiences during the winter, they were happy to display their beauty and talent on a more dignified stage, to a larger public. They bowed graciously their lovely necks for crumbs of bread and words of praise. The swans shared the ponds and also the respectful attention of the public with some ugly and greedy carps. We children, and quite often the old age pensioners, used to feed the hungry carps, with as much loving care as if they had been starving children.

By Big Pond lay the Temperance Lodge restaurant, enveloped in a dense smell of cake, substitute cream and raspberry jam. This was one of my favorite haunts, and my exhausted mother would gratefully let me visit the kind Mrs. Godenius, who lovingly stuffed me with cream buns.

To give me a change of diet, I was allowed to visit Villa Björngården, the other established restaurant in the park, painted red in the same Tyrolean style, where I fed on cream soda, toffees and sweet buns until I had made myself violently sick. My teeth turned black and decayed, and at about this time I developed a stutter and a deep bass voice.

During the summer months the well-known Chapel member Martin Lidstam used to lead the community singing on the lawn near Villa Björngården. He was a childhood friend of my father's, and I was chosen to hand Uncle Martin a bouquet of flowers, while hundreds of spectators watched with tears in their eyes. I was dressed up in tulle and bows and told to keep my mouth shut so that decayed teeth, stutter and bass voice would be concealed.

Uphill from our house, seemingly suspended in the air, was a Zoo, known as the Deer Park. It was perched on top of a hill opposite our house, and during long nights I used to listen to the piercing and plaintive shrieks of the peacocks, who must have felt as out of place in this park as a Swedish gull would feel in the jungle. Quite often I was awakened in the early hours of the morning by a donkey, who expressed his longing for the Mediterranean with screams from the bottom of his guts, squeezed through millennia of insight into darkness and poverty. The intense and piercing laments of these exotic animals produced special effects on us children. So as not to be carried away by their heart-breaking melancholy, we learned to mimic their calls. We heard them calling our names: "Geoo . . ." they called after my brother. Donkey and peacock were the most strikingly exotic inhabitants of the Zoo. For the rest there were "only" elks, deer, sheep and horses. The four of us children were mostly to be found inside the fences, looking at the spectators who in their turn watched us as if we were rare specimens of an extinct human race.

As often as we had the chance, we played in the Deer Park. I was regularly thrown by the donkey when I tried to ride him and master him. We used to pull feathers "that were loose anyway" out of the peacocks' tails, and we fed the horses. They were fat and sturdy ponies from Gotland and carthorses from the Ardennes, good, solid, democratic animals. The two brothers Rasmussen let us into the Deer Park in the afternoons after school. They were kind cattle men, whose longstanding acquaintance with the animals may have protected them from the influence of human destructiveness. On Sundays the brothers used to feed the seals before a large and appreciative crowd, and on these days especially they made it into a fine art, throwing the herrings extra high in the air before the moustachioed seals devoured them with great and audible pleasure.

The Rasmussen brothers lived in two cottages at the border of Slottsskogen, and the fabulous auntie Rill lived in another tiny house, all by herself except when I paid her a visit.

Slottsskogen was not only nature and silence or shrieks and strange animals' calls. It was the first small community where I made contact with people who were totally different from my own family.

Downhill, quite close to our house, were the estate offices (called *Gården*), where the carpenters Bergstedt and Falkman had their workshops and where I spent long hours of my lonely childhood. They were always willing to occupy themselves with me, taught me how to plane wood and use a hammer, and in order to amuse me they used to pour iron filings on a lighted match to create an atmosphere of Christmas Eve and festive sparklers.

The memory I still keep of my friends is bright and real, combined with a feeling of solidarity. Bergstedt and Falkman were rough and smooth, just like the wood they worked with, and also straight, without deceit. They ate sliced sausage in their sandwiches and sucked their coffee through lumps of sugar. They seemed more real and more human than my father's friends, drinking their whisky and soda in his study.

The kitchen garden was a place of juicy surprises that I was at first allowed to sample passively, later was told to harvest, and ended up forced to tend with hard labour. Over the years I spent large parts of my summers among the nettles and weeds with a stern father watching. "Watch what you're doing, lass—you're pulling up the plants!" he shouted while the four of us, snivelling, fought the weeds among the vegetables and the thorny bushes. We were taught to toe the line. Disciplined with the best intentions, of course.

The very first hostile relation I established with a grown-up outside my own family was with a gardener called Jansson. In reality he was kind as well as harmless, and such a slow-coach that it took him twenty minutes to say "how do you do" and half an hour to say "good bye." He was quite well known for his tardiness, and resembled in more ways than one the shiny and fat slugs who could be found eating and sleeping in the lettuce leaves.

That is to say, he was a slow-coach in everything except dealing with the mushrooms. They grew wild underneath the hedge around the kitchen garden, and when time was approaching for the first visible signs to appear, he and I stalked one another. Like a pair of silent and watchful red Indians, we tiptoed in the bushes, patiently and spitefully outwitting the opponent, so as to be able to show off our justly acquired harvest. At the same time we had a gentleman's agreement to keep all this an absolute secret. It was a silent fight for mushrooms and riches fought between the pair of us. I still remember and dream about the rich harvest—a gift, completely free of charge, as if it were a reward or an unexpected demonstration of love from the earth.

Our house was an old wooden structure, painted green with an enormous number of wardrobes and dark nooks and crannies, with an attic huge as the night and a cellar ghostlike as a grave.

The house had very few modern conveniences. I even dimly remember an earth-closet in the cellar. While the interior was rebuilt and improvements made on several occasions over the years, the children were allocated the same bedrooms all the time, my sister and I in one, my two brothers in another. My mother and father had to pass through my bedroom to reach the bathroom. In the beginning I remember the steps as light and confident, or happy and determined. As time went by they became heavier and more worried, and finally, when Death drew closer, they were full of woe and bitter lamentations, dragging their pain across the floor.

When I was still a child I used to wonder sometimes whether my father loved his precious plants and trees better than his children. He showered his tender love on the growing plants but withheld it sternly from his boisterous children.

But I suppose we all loved one another underground, through the roots, like trees, and we reached a quiet and sincere communion. I remember how my mother used to smile with happiness when she turned her tormented and tired face towards the green light filtering through the tender leaves, and she passed on her happiness to me. We shared the same happiness and it united us.

From the distance of years, my memory of Slottsskogen has a distinct solemnity, as a landscape with great contrasts of dark shadows and strong lights, a landscape which took me in when I was a small child, a very anxious little girl constructing her own precarious dream world of which she was the sovereign. In this world she was never humiliated or told to mind her manners and be good, and she was lucky to be invisible.

Being invisible was very important. I was only visible within myself, and I allowed myself to act out the plays and games that solitary children sooner or later embark on, where only I was important and accepted, just the way I was. Where words like "wicked" and "mean" exist no more than "good" and "obedient."

In this huge green palace of the imagination I had hundreds of friends and equals, and from the roots of the trees I sucked greedily both knowledge and love.

My mother was christened Debora Ifigenie Wahr Gudrun Cordelia Mignon Almuthe Renata Ximene. She was called Mignon and she died at the age of forty-eight, when I was thirteen, having lived a life filled with pain and suffering as well as vitality and creative force.

She was born in Germany, at the turn of the century. Her father, Georg Runze, was professor of Philosophy, Ethics and Theology at the University of Berlin. My grandfather wrote many books and was, supposedly, a close friend of Nietzsche's—one of the very few who were allowed to visit Nietzsche on his deathbed.

Professor Runze begot no less than fifteen children, of whom two died in infancy. He also wrote a book called *Religion und Geschlechtsliebe (Religion and Sexuality)*, which at the time caused a sensation not least because of the fact that the author was a man who lived as he preached.

My grandfather died before I was born and consequently I never had the privilege of meeting him. I know very little about him apart from some rather tall stories I was told. His photograph shows a short-sighted but handsome man with a white goatee and a high forehead. He tended to forget the names of his numerous offspring, in spite of his foresight in giving them names like Quintus, Sextus and Octavia. He had many passionate interests, among them mythology, Nordic as well as Classical, and Heroic sagas. In this respect he conformed to the tendencies of his days, especially the one that created the fertile soil from which Hitler's blond Aryans were to sprout in *"Kraft durch Freude."* I dare to suspect that my grandfather shared the prejudices of his darkening time and I am afraid that his genius did not allow him to see through and overthrow the myth of *"der Übermensch"* and the superiority of the Germanic race.

Grandfather was called Opapa, and one of his habits was to sit at the head of the long dining table with his eyes closed, lecturing on subjects that were incomprehensible as well as meaningless. During the interminable lectures, his children would quietly leave the table, one by one—unless my poor unsophisticated father happened to be visiting; he would let himself be devoutly bored from fear and reverence for Culture.

The male line on my grandfather's side is said to have consisted exclusively of Lutheran clergy.

The medical faculty of the University had requested, even before my grandfather's death, to be given his noble cranium, presumably in order to examine whether his intelligence could be measured on his skull or be revealed by bumps and enlargements on the Aryan cranium.

Consequently, when Opapa died, he lost his head, and he had to spend many years of black nights indefatigably searching for it. He found it eventually in a shoebox, left in a wardrobe in Grahlsburg, and afterwards he could rest in peace.

The story is that Opapa's head arrived at the University clinic, where it was put aside and forgotten. During the war it stayed on a shelf, collecting dust, while Opapa's lost soul searched through Grahlsburg every night. Toward the end of the war, at the collapse of Berlin, one of my uncles had the bright idea of reclaiming Opapa's head. He braved the dangers of a burning Berlin, crossing it on his bicycle to the University clinic, where he patiently searched and finally found the cranium. He then tied the shoebox with Opapa's head to his bike and with little regard for his own life, returned with the skull of the genius through a deserted Berlin, among falling bombs and hails of bullets. I see this as a fine example of the occasional triumphs of madness.

When my brother and sister-in-law visited Germany on their honeymoon in the fifties, they were shown the cranium, and a few years later I too had the pleasure of meeting Opapa face to face.

Actually, I know very little about my mother's family for the simple reason that I have always shied away from closer contact with my German origin. During the war I was penalized because my mother was German, and still I find it difficult to even mention my years in primary school, when I often was severely beaten. These wounds are still sore.

As I was growing up, I had the feeling that I alone bore the responsibility for World War II.

My grandmother, Omama, was given the title "eine Heldin des Alltags," a heroine of everyday life. The story is that she eventually lost her mind after many childbirths and severe deprivations in the shadow of her gifted spouse. She was said to have had an even temper and a tender heart.

Omama's maiden name was de Grahl, and the twenty-room family home in Lichterfelde, Berlin, took its name of Grahlsburg after her family. Her family consisted mainly of artists, journalists, authors and physicians. There is a story that Omama's grandfather was the personal physician of Napoleon but I have not been able to verify this. He supposedly lived in France under the name of Grahl, later ennobled to de Grahl. Sometimes, when I found it difficult to admit to German ancestry, I used to claim French instead. I made the most of this poor French ancestor—to be spared the shame of carrying the blood of a nation of murderers in my veins.

I can remember my mother often talking of her noble ancestry. Many members of the family like to wear their signet rings with the noble crest. Every time I look at the crest, I think I see the grin of a swindler, like a shadow behind it.

Even if she became a mental case Omama was really the heroine of the family. She bore fifteen children and brought up thirteen of them, only to lose them, one by one, during two world wars.

By way of cheering his wife and the mother of his children, the professor would urge her to look at life "sub specie aeternitatis," as he himself did. Broad perspectives create a safe distance from the problems of life.

And so it happened that we, the post-war generation, had to wash away the marks left by their passive or sometimes active guilt—very far away from "the viewpoint of eternity."

> Everywhere I go I carry the im-
> print of my mother's child-
> hood, an imprint that gives my
> life direction within the invis-
> ible prison built by earlier gen-
> erations.

My mother grew up with an intense admiration for her father and an unsatisfied longing for her mother. With so many children, the mother had little time to spare for her young daughter and female relatives were expectd to pitch in. These various aunties indulged my mother, something that caused deep resentment in the other siblings. It must have been rough to be teased by nine brothers.

All the photographs and portraits from Mama's childhood show her face with red-rimmed and tearful eyes gazing in wist-ful reverie, or occasionally with a slight smile, as if she knew secrets not to be shared. There are some photographs of her dressed in a short tunic with her heavy hair reaching her an-kles, in graceful ballet poses, wistfully extending an arm or a leg.

Mama was brought up in the same way as many of her con-temporaries in upper middle-class families. If girls showed in-tellectual aptitude, they were allowed some education, but not too much—not so much as to eliminate the feminine qualities meant for child-bearing and domestic duties.

Mama was allowed to follow Opapa's lectures and man-aged to learn, by the way, Sanskrit, several European lan-guages, and philosophy, and it is said that she mastered, for a time at least, three Indian dialects.

She was afflicted with a severe melancholy, which grew

more and more pronounced over the years. Her depressive traits combined with an overwhelming religious faith and a pessimism that at times made our home life unbearably dark. She admired and envied her sister Heide, who had a happier and lighter disposition. When Mama wanted to praise her daughters, she compared us to our Aunt Heide, just as she claimed we were the image of some ungainly, big-boned rustic relative when we made her cross.

Mama and Aunt Heide both married Swedes, fellow students in Berlin.

Mama had been in love with a young Indian, one of Opapa's students, but this was not considered a suitable match. It was on the whole not considered *comme-il-faut* to choose one's own husband.

It was the middle of the unruly twenties. My father arrived in Berlin and proceeded to take part in street-fighting. Once he stole a loaf of bread from a bakery that had been broken into by a crowd of starving people. He had spent some time in Italy in the pursuit of horticulture and love. He felt himself ready for marriage and proposed to my innocent mother.

My father was a strong-minded man, radiating sensuality— but with this sensuality kept in check by his native Swedish reserve under strict puritan control. He had a forceful personality and was handsome as well.

He eventually succeeded in enticing my mother to climb down from the exalted heights where she and the young Indian had been playing their childish games, and she took trustingly my father's firm earthy hand, whose grip was to become ever tighter over the years. My parents now started their long battle. A life filled with quarrels and rows as well as intimacy and warmth. They were both religious and romantic idealists. On the occasions when they did not quarrel, they could meet in a metaphysical dreamworld and forget, for a short while, the deadly triviality that was wearing them down, and that in time also made its mark on their children.

They were widely dissimilar in personality, with different temperament, social background and education, and they collided like terrific tropical cloud-banks. I remember frightening and fearful explosions. Both of them had been oppressed by the repressive upbringing of their day. Both of them were encumbered with a chastising God. Both of them had expectations sky-high above what was possible—but each expected completely different things from life, from each other and from their children.

Their marriage was not at all an unusual one. They lived life as they had been taught and brought the children up the same way, even if they had sworn, what seemed millions of years ago, never to perpetuate the same wrongs.

Papa was Swedish and inflexible in his demands. Mama yielded outwardly but her resentment grew and festered and eventually made her turn against her children. But when she was allowed to live in peace, with the savage wolves asleep and herself able to forget her embittered existence, she caressed us and showered all her love upon us.

Mama's religion had double standards. It could be romantically redeeming—or black and catastrophic: apocalyptic visions, fire and brimstone.

Two such conflicting personalities would never give up the fight; theirs was a life of unrelenting quarrels. Mama never had the time to pursue her artistic and intellectual inclinations. She wanted to write and paint, but my father showed no understanding at all. Her creative spirit changed to a destructive force that would destroy her in the end.

I cannot be sure to what extent all this influenced her health, but I remember her always as an invalid, in body and soul.

She contracted tuberculosis when she was thirty-nine and disappeared into a sanatorium for a whole year, and at the comparatively early age of forty-four, she developed a fatal cancer at the base of the cranium. This cancer devastated and ravaged her wretched body during four long gruesome years, with a pain that tormented her night and day. Her body was conquered by the armies of decomposition, and she, who had such a reckless lust for life, had to experience her own death by degrees before she was finally allowed to die.

All of us were changed radically by this course of events.

As children we were forced to acquire a knowledge of things too heavy to endure. We were all of us tainted inside.

Now, when I am about to describe my mother, I feel power-less. I feel as if I am walking across a minefield; I might go off with a bang at any moment and be mutilated.

This is the reason I have chosen to write two kinds of por-trait of my parents, inner and outer.

Last time—in my first book, *Väktare*—my deep anxiety, together with my need to be freed from it, wrung a description out of me. The way I then looked at my life was as if it were an evil logical consequence of my upbringing; but I do not see it like that any longer—at least not in the same way.

Society has helped to form me, a class-ridden society. I have been mutilated and battered by the same world that has muti-lated and battered my sisters and brothers.

For quite some time now I have been dwelling in the infernal regions. I have become accustomed to dark mansions and I have started to believe that I shall never see the light of day.

Today I am slowly beginning to arrange my life—what is left of it—in a world constantly changing between darkness and light.

In the old days I used to stay in the intensely burning light, surrounded by heat and life, but now I am able to enjoy warmth and light from the vantage point of a half-open cave or the shade of a tree—half out and half in. The darkness and the light have both injured me but they have healed as well.

In the world of the child, life is governed by forces that have their own irresistible laws. Feelings of love or oppression change with lightning speed. How can I possibly reproduce my childhood as it really was—today? I can only write about the memory. If I am lucky I can try to *feel myself* back to childhood.

There is one temptation I have but recently abandoned: the temptation to blame *one* person, *one* group of people, *one* injustice, to blame incessantly and at any price.

In the end it gives the wrong picture, it is not fair to other things that have molded and influenced me. It makes me false to my inner laws of morality, to the demand that I myself decide my own actions.

I may be predestined by education and environment up to a point—but not wholly.

It does not seem fair that in Sweden, where for a long time emotional life has been denied and psychology despised, when such things at last have won some recognition and interest they should fall victim to misuse and misunderstanding.

It is interesting to observe all the emotional reactions. When at long last it has become possible to help many fight their anxiety and repression, there are those who stand united in their hatred of the simple fact that some human beings cannot withstand the pressure of society without calling for help.

They tend to look for old bones of contention and describe the needy as dreamers or obscurantists. They claim that only one kind of revolution is possible, but they forget that a sick revolutionary is a danger to the cause.

It is an unfair quarrel, but there is some truth in the critiques of psychoanalysis and psychotherapy.

Varying systems of psycholanalysis, together with interest in psychology, regression to infancy and wallowing in personal misery, tend to produce some mad theories, a mixture of yoga and metaphysics from a German recipe with a touch of Reich and physical exercises, sensitivity training and wrongly interpreted primal therapy. Weekend crash courses in large country houses, with fasting and meditation on the program and therapists screwing upstairs while they tell the paying guests downstairs to practise abstinence . . . all this in order to teach people to live in groups, in a supposedly meaningful way.

What happens quite often is that somebody learns to play a

new role for a short time, learns to sit, walk, love, and speak with new body movement and voice, while inwardly the same old smog reigns. What characterizes a lot of this therapeutic mishmash is that it dissociates itself from social and political problems, shows no interest whatever in the women's movement, the conditions of the working class, and the exploitation and destructivity of capitalism on *all levels*.

All these entities are interdependent, like body and soul; and it is impossible to separate the problems of the individual from those of the rest of the world. Everything is contagious, whether it is a blemish on the skin or a deadly internal growth, something ugly and malign or good and benign.

You have to learn how to choose your path.

When I grew up we often discussed free will and moral values in general. My allegiances changed from one moment to the next, from being a devout believer in Kant's categorical imperative to a strong opponent of options, free will and guiding morality.

We, my generation, grew up under a ceiling where the nails were literally banged into our heads. Among the middle classes it was exceptional if anybody gave a thought to the importance of environment and upbringing, to psychology and well-informed tolerance, or admitted to the existence of "mitigating circumstances."

My father had muddled, conflicting ideas; for example: "so-called nerves don't exist" or "if one suffers from strained nerves, one ends up in an asylum." Once, however, when my mother suffered an almost fatal attack of gallstones he called it "just an attack of nerves." My father was not an evil man; quite the contrary. He was, as they say, an upright character, and like most such people, terribly confused.

I believe that ethical values are important and that human behavior has to conform to certain rules, of which self-awareness is the most important; also that morality cannot be seen as an independent phenomenon, complete and absolute in itself. Human conduct is varied and has to be judged accordingly; only inhuman doctrines demand set, predetermined actions regardless of circumstances.

For a long time I subscribed to the opinion that we do not possess a free will but are directed or programmed or predestined by environment and qualities inherited from parents and grandparents and even further back, by religion and history —all good and effective sponges to wipe away the burden of responsibility.

Deep inside I was stamped by my strict moral upbringing, seemingly negative and tormenting. It suited me to have a kind of redress—even if only passively—for all my sufferings. At last I was allowed to feel exculpated! Freedom from guilt was important! But at the same time I was attracted to strict and implacable socialism, which seemed to be the only ideological alternative in a completely selfish, sick and unscrupulous world.

Eventually I found certain attitudes of morality in socialism that were unconscious and unsubtle, always regarding the behavior of others—never one's own. When in despair I was driven to dissociate myself from socialism—because this generous and comprehensive doctrine had supporters who were ignorant as well as fanatical—the lack of responsibility of the uncommitted and conservative middle classes made me equally despondent.

The representatives of the middle classes were well insulated by their privileges and their firm belief that everyhing is predestined, following certain Darwinistic principles of the survival of the fittest in which the weak should accept their position at the lowest level of society, or preferably outside it; that God is on the side of those who are rich and who profit by their talents; and that tradition is the only steering wheel befitting their custom-made cars when driving on life's tough race track.

Responsibility applies primarily to one's self, one's own family, friends, property and well-being. Life is too short not to be enjoyed; that had been written already by some old

Greek. The hierarchy existed: you only had to look back in history and up toward heaven. Even liberals tried to enroll Freudian ideas in their proof, that hard work and self-seeking initiative would eradicate the problems of poverty.

I simply could not accept such rot, and I have chosen to remain a socialist, who has a lot to learn. I have found that there is much that needs changing—and renewing—in socialism.

I believe that everybody has firm ethical standards and that those who deny this have allowed grime to obscure the windows to outer and inner reality. Some of the most effective cleaning aids are self-examination and the kind of psychoanalysis that leads to self-awareness: in the strong light, through a clear reality, we can see ourselves and also our fellow human beings as we really are.

This sounds right. Perhaps it is self-evident. Trivial. It is, however, my firm belief.

My father died in February, 1978, at the age of seventy-nine. It had been my pleasure to make his acquaintance when I was adult, and that made him a friend, an intimate friend more than the father I remember from my childhood. The friend and my father were two different persons.

Throughout my childhood my father played the role of somebody who admonished and educated. I cannot remember him as a person; besides, he seemed always to be absent: even when he was present physically, he was hidden behind a newspaper or busy with something or other. I was allowed to wait with his slippers in the evenings and also to massage his legs when he was tired after too much walking in the forest, and that was how I could steal brief moments to be with him. He used to let me taste his whisky and soda, in deepest secret, when Mama was not looking.

As I grew older, the contact between us increased, and when I returned to Sweden in 1970 and moved to "Victoria," my father started visiting more and more often. For the first time we could talk, really talk—nothing like the lectures he used to treat us to at mealtimes. At this time he was almost completely blind. He suffered from glaucoma and had had several unsuccessful operations. His blindness had progressed very rapidly and during our walks in the forest my eyes had to do more and more of the seeing. He had an odd sort of near-sightedness that could suddenly stop him in his tracks and let him point out a magnificent mushroom that had escaped my notice. Or maybe his intuition told him about the mushroom. He had spent all his life outdoors and never felt like a stranger. Depression set in and increased with his progressive blindness, and to counteract this I had the idea to ask him to record his life story on tape.

Intermittently, during two years, I was allowed to handle the tape-recorder while my father was talking. He had always suffered from insomnia, and as he grew older he only needed a couple of hours of sleep at night. He told me that at last he felt that his sleepless hours were of some use; he spent his nights putting his "book," his life, into words. He conjured up pictures from the past and the memories came willingly forth, the painful and the pleasant. He treated them like children, brushing their clothes and making them tidy. Some of them behaved very well and others played nasty tricks on him.

All this seemed to give my father a new lease on life, and his strong emotions often made him cry, unexpectedly and helplessly, as if he had been ambushed by life and time, as if he again was living through an event that had once shattered him—but at a time when he was not allowed to show his feelings.

This has proved invaluable to me and helped to reconcile me to much in my own life—most of all to my father. My love for him grew after years of bitterness; and it made me understand that he was not only the man I knew as a child, or rather, the man I did not know, but also somebody different, who lived a life of whose existence his children knew nothing, a sad and rich life, a life ruled by a strict superego and at the same time gentle and bewildered, filled with anxiety and faith.

Papa often compared himself to a patchwork quilt, a mixture of contradictory impulses and feelings, ideas and aspirations. He crouched, like most of us, deep inside his own labyrinth, finding it difficult to escape.

When Papa was seventy-five years old, I threw him a ball of thread, and day by day we approached one another through the labyrinth.

My father remained a proud man all his life; but his childhood had left its marks on him just as it has on his children. He never forgot his poor childhood and was humbly grateful for his later achievements. Like many parents, he kept telling us that we must never forget what his childhood had been like.

Papa's surname was Karlsson, but when some of the numerous offspring decided to change it by deed poll, he chose Axelsson, and I loved him for that. He did not aspire to gentility through his name, and plain Karlsson became plain Axelsson. No point in making oneself important; and anyway, before God we are all equals: Svensson and Lefvermärd, Karlsson and Tunbjär. When it rains, we all get wet and when the sun shines we feel warm. Life can be straightforward like that. Sometimes.

My father was born on a smallholding in Sörmland and was one of six children. My grandfather belonged to Chapel, preached sometimes and looked after Sunday school in the parish.

My grandparents, whom I never met, managed to eke out their meager existence from the yield of their seven acres and the milk from their few cows.

"We were never poor," Papa used to say, "but we were short of everything." The household also included an ox, everybody's favorite. Papa's memories of his childhood are strongly reminiscent of Ivar Lo-Johansson's descriptions of conditions of life among the farmhands, but he was always careful to point out the difference between farmhands and small-holders.

Everybody in the family had to work extremely hard, and the portrait Papa paints of his mother is very touching—but also heart-sickening. Love and admiration shone from his eyes when he described her inhuman work-load, her mildness, soft heart, and sweet temper. His father was a taciturn puritan, a work-worn and god-fearing man who lived in constant fear of hell. He had an uncompromising belief in sin and its punishment, with the result that worldly pleasures like visits to the cinema, the theatre, and even to secular concerts were forbidden. Words of encouragement, or in fact, any words at all, were only used in church services and as admonitions.

Papa's upbringing was harsh, and the only toys he ever possessed he had made himself.

He always felt like an outsider and vulnerable as well, without knowing why. He showed musical talent and early learned to play the flute very well, just as he later learned to play the organ. He played in chapel already at the age of twelve. "The congregation could only see a small head nodding above the organ."

Everybody in the family had some musical talent. One uncle, Elof, built violins and once won second prize as a violinmaker at an exhibition in Stockholm.

Only my father was supposed to have real intellectual ability, and since he had shown an interest in plants and trees (as it were, near at hand) he was apprenticed to a gardener. "A gardener had status, and to be a student of gardening meant you had prestige; it was considered a good stepping stone in climbing the peaks of life."

As my father was telling me about his life, and primarily about his childhood, he was apt to be upset and very bitter. He relived everything as if he were a child; even his choice of words became strange and rather awkward, he who was normally a master of wording.

The father I remember from my own childhood had no past. He had never cried as a child, he had never been punished, and he understood nothing of his own children—at least, that is how I felt, because there was no connection between the father-figure of my childhood and the man I learned to know in my middle age. On the other hand, there was a clear line from his chastising father to the way he chastised his own children, in the way he withheld praise from us just as his father had withheld his praise.

His father's forbidding edicts, severity, and unrelenting manner toward him was mirrored in his manner toward us.

If I could liken him to an open ice-cold ocean, there were also occasional warm streams, where we felt the mildness that he later described as his mother's main attribute, and he showed that he had inherited traits from both parents.

He raised himself very slowly from the grinding poverty of the small-holder's life. He had always dirt on his hands and the intense blueness of the sky in his eyes. He dreamed and he grew like an oak, every year pressing his roots deeper into the earth of harsh reality that was seldom prosaic, gloomy or poor, but often cruel and violent with the irresistible force and sensual poetry that is contained in nature.

Papa worked as a gardener and as shop assistant while he studied for his A levels, and later when he had enrolled in college to train as a landscape architect. During his student days abroad he worked as foreman for giant projects in Italy, where he worked up a sweat in the cypress groves and fell in love with the young ladies of the manor. His life was "efficient," in his own words; he was "vigorous" and passionate, full of enthusiasm and pride. But poverty was always there, present and past, burning like fire. Wrongs were rarely forgiven and never forgotten. If we ever asked his pardon for any kind of misdemeanor, he usually said "there is no point in asking forgiveness. Improve yourself instead."

Papa became in time an authority in his field. At the time of my birth he had been promoted to garden architect for Slottsskogen, the largest park area in Gothenburg, and a few years later he become the garden architect for the entire city, almost always working indoors, at his drawing board or in meetings with various committees, having to decide how Gothenburg should look, all year round. Sundays he usually went hunting, one of the vices my mother found difficult to condone, although the venison he brought home must have been a welcome addition to the meager fare during the war years.

He travelled to conferences, became a member of various societies like "Odd Fellow" and "Rotary," another thing my mother disliked. For him, though, it was proof of his success. He had become a pillar of society, but the soil still clung to his remarkably beautiful hands.

His hands were big but supple. I could never understand how he was able to handle delicate plants in the most intricate operations without fumbling and getting his big fingers in the way. He was also an accomplished amateur musician, playing the flute and the piano. His hands had developed a sensitivity that is common among the blind, and during the long process while he was becoming almost totally blind they became his main aid. During the last years of his life he applied himself to advanced carpentry and to making exquisite parcels.

He could wrap a parcel like nobody else.

It is quite common to idealize one's parents, but I don't think I can be accused of that; rather the reverse. Most people have, in my experience, some inherent trait, a gesture or personal quirk or habit that expresses his or her tenderness and affection, even if these qualities are normally well hidden. With my father it was his way of wrapping parcels.

I left home at seventeen and only came home for short visits afterwards. I often felt lonely and lost, especially so every time I had to return to Stockholm. Relations with the rest of the family were strained, though I wished, fervently, never to feel *de trop* or misunderstood ever again. When the time came for me to leave, Papa and I had not really talked, and he had never, somehow, been able to show affection or appreciation —by this time I had seventeen years of unfulfilled longing to be loved by him—that is when he would start on his beautiful parcels, usually several of them, with picnic food and fruit for the journey, often intricate arrangements with flowers and fragile things, ingeniously held together with string, plaited to make them easy to carry. He was always gentle and patient, lovingly fitting the different objects together like a puzzle.

He made the bed comfortable for the sandwiches, pulled the blanket over the cookies, gave the apples their good-night kiss and plumped the pillows under some old handkerchiefs he was giving me as a present. He wanted the parcel filled to capacity, so full in fact that it barely closed, which would give him the opportunity to start making it all over again, even more intricate and ingenious, with tissue paper protecting the fragile things, just like the gentle pressure on the arm as support when helping somebody across the street.

This solemn ritual brought out his strong paternal love with touching intimacy. Most of all he loved to pack my suitcase, but I seldom dared to ask him; after all, he was my father and I did not want to flaunt my possessions shamelessly.

As his blindness progressed, his ability to make parcels diminished, but instead a new emotional element was added: he was not alone, he could collaborate. His blindness brought him closer to all of us, and at last he was allowed to show openly his need of care and love. For example, he could at one moment ask for the butter knife he supposedly could not see and a minute later he had forgotten that he "couldn't see" the butter knife and could start paring the cheese or reaching for the milk jug with absolute precision. He still had, on occasion, some locomotor vision and near-sightedness—but his failing sight very often let him down in earnest. As soon as he found out how much it pleased us to help him, he used his helplessness as a means to accept our love and affection.

To make his parcels he had to ask me to hand him whatever he wanted to pack and then ask me if it was well placed. It usually was, and our dialogue about the parcel and its contents went on and could be translated to mean: "My little girl, your old father is not long for this world, and though he never was able to express his feelings for you and the other children—he always loved you...."

Yes, Father, we knew—and we were fully aware that he had devoted ninety percent of his life to his family, to the extent that he almost lost his own identity. He was spiritual guide and justice of the peace, and he helped us all with his tolerance, understanding and love to cope with difficult and burdensome relations.

He took part in our lives, the good and the bad parts—but he never intruded and was quite happy to live in peace with his second wife. Real peace, he claimed, he would not expect until he was firmly in his grave, because even if his children had one after the other managed to cut the umbilical cord, he was still as firmly tied to them. He loved us more than his life.

It is now the end of September. A sunny, light and serious day. The forest is bursting with chanterelles and apples are falling heavily off their branches. I am so intensely reliving the past that I sometimes cannot be sure whether I am really in Slottsskogen or here, in Victoria.

If it were only possible to bypass childhood, quickly and simply, to grow up and to understand. But just as it is difficult to live through childhood it is equally difficult to relive the experiences when writing about them. My childhood is like a tight cork in a magical bottle, and only when I release the cork and let the demon out will I be able to fulfill my own wishes. I feel like a spring flood that's dammed up. I am a catastrophe of nature that is held back.

Last night I dreamed of my old home in Slottsskogen. As often in my dreams, the house is completely and frighteningly dark. If it is ever peopled, they creep about, barely visible in the weak light from the street. Most often I am completely alone until somebody enters, somebody destructive.

In this dream the house was in a state of decay, and my dominant feeling was indescribable fear mixed with anger. I begin to suspect that this constant darkness in my dreams indicates that I have literally tried to black out childhood.

It is significant that I was falling asleep last night thinking that my childhood had never existed or rather that I myself had never existed as a child.

In the dream I was back in my old home and my mother was back too, either from the hospital or from death. She was alive, but so weak that anything might precipitate her death. My parents were together upstairs, my father very old but forceful, serious and menacingly warning and he definitely did not want to listen to what I was about to say to my mother and pretended to busy himself with something or other. Two of the other children appeared for a while and then disappeared. I was terribly upset and could feel, through my sleep, my heart beating so hard it almost burst.

There was something I had to ask my mother even though I sensed that my question might kill her again. I plucked up my courage and shouted: "Did you love the others more than you loved me?" She could not speak but nodded instead. Wild with rage I shouted that she lied. I was trying so hard to convince her, as if my own life depended on this "last" answer.

Was it not true that she had written in her diary how much she loved me? In letters? At this point in the dream she whispered weakly that she had loved me—but only when I was a good and submissive baby. Crying with agitation and despair I tried to convince her, explain, make her change her mind. How could it be my fault? It was instead she who had abandoned me, was it not? She had simply disappeared from home.

In my dream I was five years old, and while I was raging against her, she became invisible. I can remember my precocious choice of words when I turned to my parents and said, "do you not realize what a tragedy it is for a small child to be left alone?" Throughout the dream my fear grew stronger. My father had disappeared after a last look of reproach and hate, and my mother had died again. The darkness around me had become inpenetrable and now came Mama's revenge. Objects and lamps were thrown about the room, and I ran screaming to the kitchen, which was also pitch black. My youngest brother was there; he seemed confused as if he were drugged. I begged him to go down to the basement to mend the fuses but he refused, saying he was afraid of falling down the stairs. He could not see anything either, and somebody had poured alcohol down there, which might catch fire. I felt a moment of security with my brother, which was splintered by my sister, who brought back my anger and despair. I asked her if it was really true that Mama had loved her best and she said "Of course" with nonchalant and supercilious calm before she disappeared. My brother came back toward me to console me, but before reaching me he also became invisible. While I was loking for him everywhere, the flying objects had started hitting me about the head and chairs were moving about. I can remember feeling near death from fright and fear, feeling cruelly deceived, abandoned and exposed. I felt I was being murdered by objects thrown by invisible members of my own family. At the same time I felt an overwhelming sorrow for my brother; I wanted to help him but knew he could never become visible again.

I woke up with my heart beating hard and fast, feeling close to destruction. I slowly calmed down after this dream that is possibly the most difficult I have ever experienced, emotionally. By and by I found explanations to problems that I have never previously been able to solve. The explanations are my own and I cannot be sure that they fit—but I am quite confident that the dream in itself is a fairly explicit summary of the most difficult conflicts of my childhood. It is possible that one single analysis, one interpretation, my own, might suffice to penetrate the main problems of my childhood, but that one interpretation would exclude the other, light side that existed simultaneously as vital and warm protection.

I am the youngest of four children, born when my mother was thirty-four years old, after eight years of marriage. The four years preceding my birth had seen a family with three children, leading a fairly harmonious life before this last "intruder" came into their world that was a well-functioning collective.

Mama was already getting exhausted from looking after the children and the big house entirely without help. I spent my early days out of doors in a large pram, whatever the weather. Neither blizzards nor thunderstorms would persuade her to bring me indoors, as she was firmly convinced that fresh air was good for babies. I have seen photographs of my pram with twenty inches of snow on the hood, under which I probably was trying to figure out whether I had really been born.

Mama considered me an easy and sweet-tempered child, quietly crowing to myself. When I started sucking my thumbs, my little hands were enclosed in clothbags, which I tore and bit until they were bloodied. As I was growing up I became aware of the advantages of "goodness," and I practiced it with great success on my parents, thereby gaining their affection and at the same time trying to avoid the older childrens' teasing by submissiveness. This turned out to be a miscalculation: it provoked them to anger. My parents increased the older childrens' animosity by constantly holding me up as "a little ray of sunshine" and a good example to them. I think their spontaneous reaction to me had been affection and curiosity toward their new playmate.

When they were provoked by my precocious innocence, their teasing and pinching started. They had to find out how long I could keep my mask of frightened innocence. That taught me early in life some guerilla tactics, counterattack when neither of the parents was watching. This could be very dangerous, because revenge without witnesses can be brutal; it also helped me to develop a system of defense and attack which kept pace with the growing family repression. Most of the time I was scared stiff, scared of the scolding heaped on the older children, which sounded like doomsday trumpets and volcanic eruptions, scared of the quarrels between the parents. I felt as if all these quarrels were my fault somehow, and feared they would kill one another.

The older children teased me affectionately but unmercifully and put me firmly in my place. My sister, who had frequently been beaten with a leash, was certainly not entirely happy about my arrival. The well-mannered little sister stole the show from her and the boys, and made them seem noisy and naughty.

Of all things on earth, the most coveted was approval by our parents. In retrospect it is easy to see that we as children should have kept a united front against the adults who, with thoughtless cruelty and "the best intentions," played us one against the other. But we were only joined in solidarity when one of us had been given an extra hard beating, something that most often seemed to fall to my sister's lot. I have always felt deep compassion for her who, as the oldest, had to bear the brunt of my parents' neurotic experiment in child-rearing. When my turn came they had spent their force, and only minor instances of corporal punishment remained—apart from the scolding, of course. I don't know if a more just distribution of chastisement could have helped to make me a sharer in the family unity. As it was, I always felt like an outsider and never a welcome member. I learned from the beginning the art of self-effacement. When this art passed into its opposite, into self-manifestation—then came the time for self-chastisement, physical obliteration. Suicide.

The older children were constantly compared to heroic figures. My oldest brother was expected to be a new Nietzsche and a great philosopher. He had been born apparently dead and had to be beaten into life—as if the little body had been fully aware of what was waiting outside and had wanted to return to the mild and soft darkness.

My sister was chosen to be a saint. She was expected to be a marvel of moral stature, a possessor of talent and inner as well as outer beauty. My youngest brother was the financial genius, as he had shown an early interest in business by selling our pears in school. I was supposed to be the little sunshine with a vague artistic talent.

My oldest brother is a physician, specializing in ears, as if he unconsciously has wished to force deaf ears to hear and understand what children have to say. My sister trained as a teacher and proceeded to maintain order in her classes as we had been disciplined at home, but her memory was good and she developed psychological understanding instead of punishment. My youngest brother turned to business, as my mother had correctly predicted, but he sometimes gave away his proceeds in protest to this obedience.

When I was five years old, my mother's tuberculosis was diagnosed and she had to go to a sanatorium for treatment. This year has left few memories, but my dream brought back a legacy of deep-rooted fear. The three older children went to school, but I had a nanny to look after me. She wanted to see me cry and would say that my mother had gone away, never to return. As soon as she had succeeded in making me desperate, she would say that "it was all a game" and try to make me laugh. The whole thing was turned into a hysterical game that amused her and other spectators. I learned early that feelings are exploitable and lost confidence in the language used by adults. I learned to see through the words and at the same time lost my feeling of security.

When I went to visit Mama at the sanatorium, she often told ghost stories, and this habit continued after she had returned home. She had heard the rattling of chains, seen luminous apparitions, predicted the death of several of the patients. Mama's sixth sense had generally been working overtime during her stay in hospital. She always told her stories at night, in front of the fire, and it was scary to go to bed afterwards in the dark. I can remember that my father sometimes tried to protest—he probably realized that these were not suitable bedtime stories for small children—but I cannot really judge how significant they were. My childish scepticism shielded me except when Mama made the connection between an act of disobedience and its concomitant punishment. With dangerous innocence she was apt to say; "A clear conscience has nothing to fear."

When I think about it now, I am convinced that what hit me hardest was the fact that she simply disappeared, and that also changed me profoundly. When she returned, my need of affection made itself doubly felt and was something my weak and tired mother would find increasingly difficult to satisfy, just as my tiring demands stirred her conscience to ever greater despair.

At this time they started to dispatch me to various places in Slottsskogen, to summer camp with the older children or to the Gullanders on the West Coast. "You somehow didn't count. You never seemed to be present," one of my relatives said at my father's funeral.

The "little ray of sunshine" had turned into a hailstorm. Mama found me changed and difficult: her good little girl had run away. Words like "house of correction" and "psychiatrist" were mentioned. I started having attacks of fainting and vomiting, which worried her, mostly because I dirtied my clothes, and that caused her to punish me. Several years later, a physician gave her an acceptable explanation, namely that my attacks were caused by a form of epilepsy. On hearing this diagnosis, she tried to make amends and asked my forgiveness; but this scared me and was also incomprehensible, as rows with subsequent punishments seemed perfectly normal to me.

Another possible explanation of my attacks is that I wanted to get her attention and thereby her love; but I never regained her attention.

I started school inauspiciously and from the beginning found it difficult to get on with the other pupils and my teachers, which showed in my poor marks. My younger brother was like myself "a nervous child." My sister and older brother were back in mama's favor; they were more adult and easier to handle.

When the war started, Mama became severely depressed and lived in a constant state of anxiety. Relations between the parents seemed strained.

I can remember quarrels lasting days or even weeks on end, when one or the other of them stayed behind a locked door. Papa sometimes brought his gun and threatened to shoot himself, while Mama knelt, praying to God. We children talked between ourselves about our parents' imminent divorce; we were united in our despair and often pleaded with them, steadfastly and bravely trying to solve their inexplicable conflicts. I became unbearably precocious and did not rid myself of this stamp until many years later.

In reality, Mama lost her life several years before she died. Her cancer, lymphatic sarcoma, grew along the base of the skull and further into the brain and caused her immense, unbearable pain that morphine could not alleviate.

Against this dark background I can see her portrait in light. She was full of love and a humanity that made her sensitive to the problems of others and also responsive to everybody and everything. She had no strength left for her own family—especially not after her health deteriorated; but her need to manifest what was good in her, to give herself unstintingly to those who believed in her, who accepted her love and loved her in return—that need caused her to neglect husband and children.

She constantly suffered from a bad conscience toward us, which made her feel guilty and angry with herself and with us.

In the battle of wills with her husband, she had lost her self-confidence, and in the picture of herself she saw reflected in the mirror her family held up she saw a monster. She, who wanted to be good and beautiful, could only be ill.

Of the four of us, my sister was closest to her during the last years of her life. This was a mortal blow to me. Mama would not even pretend that she needed me or loved me. She could not even bear to look at me. "Take that child out of my sight," she said, over and over again. She seemed to project on me the evils she had to go through; she even saw maggots crawl out of my face. I understood nothing and was desperately unhappy. I, who had been her sunshine? How could everything change like that?

My sister gradually took over the household. She managed to go to grammar school, take over the role as mother and look after Mama, all at the same time. I think that she had bitterly resented me during earlier years when I had been close to Mama, and during Mama's last years when she regained her love, it made her doubly anxious to please. It seemed as if they had a secret pact—I had to be sacrificed.

The outer and the inner theater!

By and by I discovered that the sharpest pain could be turned into the very opposite with the help of fantasy or by switching to another existence. I termed these two states the outer and the inner theater. In the outer theater, life's normal atrocities and dramas occurred, intense and merciless, but my mechanism of defense was too undeveloped to take the strain. I started to counteract this strain by creating my own world. The audience in my inner theater was always warm, understanding, friendly and appreciative just as it was critical, scornful, punishing and dangerous in the outer.

All my life I have had my inner theater. When I was young, it served as the secure haven where I automatically fled for help. As I grew older, I found it more and more difficult to separate the two theatres.

My safe haven failed sometimes, and I had no dreams and plays of compensation to act. The wings were empty and quiet, the audience had left me alone on the big stage—desperate and alone, deprived of my protection and talking to an empty room.

I found a way out of this situation. With the help of a glass of wine, I could entice the audience back and make the play progress without problems and with the repartee flitting like happy swallows between my different selves.

During many years I had very little contact with reality. I lived separated from life, in my private world, but exposed and vulnerable to real life in my outer theater, where I never learned to act well. People around me have met a succession of actresses instead of the real me. A deep-rooted fear has helped me to switch intuitively and with lightning speed to whatever personality would suit any given situation.

I acted a role as a defense against spite and violence or to get some support in order to survive.

Before I could accept anybody as a friend—friend of the real me—this remarkably strong person had to be involved in some of my complicated plays and at the same time stay outside, be audience in both theaters, be more observant and more wise than I and still love me, in spite of my hidden aggression and sometimes threatening behavior. I possess few intimate friends—but those I have remain faithful.

Thanks to my friends I have slowly had the courage to turn to reality—when the plays were finished, when the theater closed and went into liquidation, when wine and food and play-acting no longer could give relief, when reality was there, in the wings: implacable, revengeful and challenging.

I had help to learn walking, groping my way like a blind person, and felt liberated by embracing real life. The inner theater exists in the outer and vice versa; real life-pain contains its own relief, and evil corresponds to good in reality. Life itself is an ever-changing, entertaining theater for those who do not remain outsiders or shun it.

I have almost entirely forgotten my first plays for the inner theater, although I am fairly confident that they were magnificent fairy tales as consolation for the real-life dramas. I remember that, being the youngest in a large chaotic family with numerous friends and relations, I was often forgotten.

One time, when we all went Christmas shopping, I disappeared, and my parents looked in vain in the jostling crowds. Santa Clauses, whistles, music and other crying children drowned my screams when I found myself lost in the general chaos, crying buckets and howling with abandon.

Somebody took pity on me, took me into a tobacconist's shop and started asking questions. Eventually I calmed down and the police were called.

The play started on the inner scene. The audience was crowding in, smiling and friendly. I became the focus of attention, my photograph was to be published in tomorrow's newspaper. The people in the shop were going to look after me, in order to punish my uncharitable parents, and reward me with sweets and cakes.

Eventually my parents appeared, direct from Reality. They shouted and carried on and were generally disagreeable in front of my audience. I was ashamed of them and of myself. What was everybody going to think? Who were they going to believe—me or them? I needed another play to help me solve that conflict and the fear.

The next time they lost me was at my brother's confirmation. Everybody departed on a train for Kungsbacka and left me standing on the platform, small and alone, dressed in white from top to toe. The sensible station master stopped me from throwing myself onto the moving train. He made me wait for the next train for Kungsbacka, hoping that the parents would be coming back for their lost luggage. I spent the next hour dreaming up a play about a little girl going to visit fat and good-humored people in the country, on a farm, where I was going to milk the cows and eat lovely home-made buns.

My exhausted Papa arrived from Reality to the Central Station, just as the next train was about to leave with his milking, dreaming daughter on her way to billowing fields and newly made buns.

Papa was embarrassed and suggested that I should board the train first instead of last.

It has happened that the inner theater has been lured on to the unfriendly stage of the outer theater.

The older children once had to take me to a public outdoor swimming pool, very much against their wishes as they had hoped to escape looking after the ray of sunshine. I was sternly told to stay at the shallow end, sitting like a silly little frog among the babies while the others threw themselves in at the deep end, diving, splashing, floating, swimming like fish and having a lot of fun.

I must have been about five and I could not swim. But never mind. In my "inner" pool I was a good swimmer and I could jump head first from the diving board. My splendid performance was much appreciated and everybody applauded. While all this took place in my inner pool, I had moved toward the outer pool and in Reality I threw myself fearlessly at the deep end and sank like a stone. When I woke up, people were leaning over me, not to applaud but to make me vomit.

I have been throwing myself between different pools, Fantasy and Reality, diving in at the deep end or sitting in the shallow, half drowned or dry, admired champion swimmer one minute and the next a forsaken child, feeling unsuccessful and forgotten.

I cannot say why all this reminds me of a journey I once undertook with a friend to Lido di Jesolo. My memory insists that I write about it; maybe it has some obscure relevance.

A few years ago friends lent us a flat in Lido di Jesolo. We left Sweden at the end of summer for Italy, where the heat was unbearable.

I had been living with Olle for a long time. We were by now good friends; passion had cooled during the last years. We had gone through many crises when it had seemed as if we would never be able to resume our relations, whether in the physical or the spiritual sense.

We tried naively to solve our problems with new acquisitions. First crisis brought a small dog, second crisis a pair of canaries, later on one more small dog when the first had puppies. We surrounded ourselves with lots of interesting potted plants and at the fifth or sixth crisis we were ready to try our luck with a Chinese rice bird. We sometimes went away together to find out if a different climate could give new life to frozen feelings or just to find the time to examine our relations and try to find a cure.

The pattern was familiar. Ever since childhood I had fled from reality and from the strain of the outer theatre to the inner, trying to drown my sorrows with a variety of devices that caused headaches and other ills. I knew no other pattern of life, was a stranger to reality, alienated.

By closing my eyes I could change my life. I could step out from the balcony on the fifth floor and expect to find soft grass only one step away.

We arrived in Lido on a suffocatingly close day, did not find a taxi and had to walk from the station, several kilometers, with all our luggage. Lido is the ugliest of resorts, and it was crammed with German tourists, walking and eating their way up and down the promenade when they were not sitting and eating in Italian taverns, transformed into German beerhalls and Bavarian restaurants. The air reeked of liver sausage and I was close to tears of disappointment. The whole scene was an orgy in bad taste and looked like a gigantic outdoor brothel.

The Italians were speaking German and the Germans spoke an unattractive mixture of Italian and English. Frightened tourists from other smaller countries tried to flatten themselves against the walls when Tyrolean families of seven or eight members came yodelling by, enormous, cheerful and full of hard currency. Without a doubt, Lido belonged to them; and although I don't grudge any man his happiness as long as it does not directly infringe on my own, this German happiness did infringe. All traces of Italy had been swept away and been replaced by German paraphernalia: the decor was a disgusting German synthetic baroque, the waitresses and waiters were dressed in German national costume. I expected Goebbels to come limping, by, but he had sent his children instead. Most men bore a striking resemblance to a beefy Franz Josef Strauss—faces shining of beer, sauerkraut and pork fat.

We barricaded ourselves for the next few days in the flat, which was pleasant, almost beautiful, small and comfortable with a lovely view of the sea. The view avoided the beach, crawling with German bathers like a pit of hungry and curious grubs. Further out in the bay we could see the big ships, without having to notice the oil pollution. The smog toward Mestre could be seen as a light morning mist.

We had been shocked on arrival and had to calm down before we dared to start exploring. Olle went out looking for an Italian grocery and came back, exhausted, after several hours—with salami, spaghetti and a bottle of Chianti.

In some diabolic way I felt trapped and guilty. My German childhood had finally caught up with me, baying dogs and all.

We lived on spaghetti and salami so as to be spared knödel, wurst and kalbmaulsallat.

I tried going to the beach but left soon after diving in among condoms, excrement and plastic bags. In despair I tried to reach the cleaner water farther out by swimming fast, but that was immediately seized upon as a new game by eight competitive Germans. There seemed nothing to do but to withdraw to my balcony, where I fried and boiled during the hottest hours—far from water but determined to acquire a tan. The beauty of a lovely tan: maybe that could do something toward improved relations?

Olle stayed in the shade, ashen pale and sweaty, panting over his book, quiet and withdrawn. We ate and drank a lot each night, working hard to create a joyful holiday atmosphere.

Soon I had withdrawn to my inner theatre, with the flat and balcony as backdrop to my fantasies, and we rarely left our stronghold. We had succeeded in finding an Italian restaurant at the outskirts of town where we would surreptitiously sneak after dark, breathlessly listening for German pursuers with their loud bursts of laughter. We felt like conspirators, like resistance fighters during a war, temporarily dominated by Germans. The Battle of Lido di Jesolo was imminent and we had formed a small group of comrades and brave soldiers. Our flat with the grandiose view was headquarters, across the street from the enemy's luxury hotel, where extravagant cars were stopping all the time, unloading Nazis.

Olle and I entered into our new meaningful existence with courage, commitment and enthusiasm. Now and again Olle had to sneak out to get provisions from the prohibited Italian shop, hidden by ruins, where only the correct password would let you in.

We made love, passionately and breathlessly, before we had to part when duty called us to other important tasks. Olle had to tear himself away, say farewell with the stiff upper lip he used to combat his weakness and go off to the bank to get the money we needed for spaghetti and weapons.

More and more Germans arrived. The final battle between the partisans and the brown-shirts was imminent. Risking our lives, we went for our farewell dinner to a small Italian restaurant where we had never seen any Germans and where Italian was still spoken.

Conversation over the grilled meatballs was whispered and intense. We pretended not to understand the waiter addressing us in German. "Nein, kein bier" he asked helplessly. We asked him to lower his voice and tried to find out if he was with us or with the enemy. After a substantial tip, he finally started speaking his mother tongue and we ordered another bottle of Chianti, with a sigh of relief.

We felt that our last night was a solemn occasion. Instead of hurrying home, we took a walk through town with all the risks it implied. We managed to escape a pair of dead drunk American sailors, who tried to drag us into the restaurant *Der frohe Piltz*, and later we witnessed a frightening scene between a German colonel and the Italian policeman he had tried to run over.

Sitting on our balcony, far from the barren North, we saw the moon sail across the sky on this unforgettable night, when we had succeeded in avoiding the seventh crisis with the help of alienation, imagination and good will—on both sides.

Fatigue was setting in, though. Swedish pallor and gloom leaned nonchalantly in the doorway of the headquarters. Reserve and surfeit were waking up from their slumber. My slimness disappeared and in its place the usual obesity. My hair showed gray. Words sounded harsher and seemed to stick in the throat. Our embraces felt like Monday morning after a boozy weekend. In short, our strength was ebbing.

My inner theatre had closed down due to hangover, but there remained a spark of life in our holiday and in us. The moon kept rolling along and the music had a deafening and

German ring to it, bellowing from the hotel, where the soldiers were having a ball.

We held hands before we had to take the train to the unknown—or worse, back to the well known.

I had washed my underclothes and hung them on the balcony to have them nice and clean for the journey home. The Sambuca had made us tired and dull and we went to bed, feeling a bit dejected, and fell asleep to the strains of "Die Fahne hoch."

Some hours later I woke up, coughing, thick smoke everywhere. The Germans had attacked. I saw SS soldiers entering the house—with boots and leather jackets. Coughing and utterly confused, I shook Olle awake and he shot up, shouting "Fire," staggering round the flat. Smoke was pouring in through the windows and french doors, but there was no fire and all seemed quiet. Looking from the balcony, I could see what had caused the smoke. A black poisonous deadly fog lay like a heavy blanket on the town, the smog from industrial Mestre. I could not breathe and my eyes were streaming with tears. Olle implored me to come in and close the door.

Through the curtain of fog I heard the starting motors of the luxurious cars belonging to the Nazis, and I heard their agitated voices. The Germans were retreating. Victory was ours, as we waited for daybreak . . . if there was to be a break of day.

In the morning, through the dark haze, as if all the locusts of Egypt were there blackening the sky, we could see and listen to the bustling town. My underclothes, white the night before, looked daringly black on the washing line, our lungs felt like the entire Ruhr district, and the seventh crisis was approaching, without mercy.

This time we were properly stuck, no shut-off button and no inner theatre. We had it all in front of us: Reality, alienation, pollution, madness, our inhuman future in the holy name of rational capitalism.

A naughty girl!

Parents of my generation had learned their lesson that children should be reshaped, kneaded like dough, fashioned to a different mold from the one given at birth.

Straighten the crooked, caution the independent, lock up the freedom-loving and punish the self-willed. The more independent the child, the more control is needed.

Parents don't have easy options. Edicts and advice change minute by minute. What was dangerous yesterday is considered good today. Parents, who have themselves been guinea pigs to an earlier generation, experiment on their own live material, leaving pockmarks like small and invisible craters in the soul.

Babies want regular habits, feed them every four hours. No, babies should be left undisturbed to wake of their own accord.

Children ought to learn early self-reliance. No, they should be led as long as possible and be given a sense of security. They must not be allowed to masturbate. Yes, masturbating is good for them. One must not scold and shout at children. On the contrary, be "natural" and don't hide your feelings. Children can be shocked by looking at naked adult bodies. Children ought to learn at an early age to come to terms with sensual and physical manifestations. Be yourself! Control yourself!

Bringing up their children, my parents shared a basic moral principle, stemming from their religiosity. Both had firm standards, at least in theory, but in practice they preferred different character traits.

Mama looked kindly on intelligence and talent, joined to

piety and innocence of mind. She liked beauty but punished signs of vanity, like anyone trying to embellish nature. Purity of soul and thought was high on her list and she was wont to talk of "nobility of the soul."

Papa was maniacally obsessed with punctuality, discipline, cold showers, getting up at the crack of dawn even on Sundays, managing one's homework and finishing all the food on one's plate. Boys were allowed a reasonable amount of cheek, classified as manliness; wild horseplay out of doors. Girls were expected to show complete submissiveness, seriousness and application to domestic virtues. My parents brought with them, in invisible knapsacks from their respective homes, the same character-traits they were looking for and expected to implant in the next generation.

The tears were conveniently forgotten, just as the pain of beatings, of "the purification of the dross," of "straightening out" nature was forgotten or at least altered in memory when their theories were put into practice.

I conformed for a long time to the good girl and the ray of sunshine bit. A puppy is rewarded with pats on the head, words of encouragement and edible treats, and I was rewarded for my silence, obedience and passivity with suitable spiritual and material goodies.

When I changed, when nature started showing signs of defects, weakness of character, propensity for thieving and lying, when I dirtied myself, started losing my German hairclips "unobtainable in Sweden," became defiant, nervous, impatient, started having fainting-fits, vomited, wet myself, had nightmares and a wild imagination, when all these cracks in my nature showed up, I was no longer the sunshine and a good example to the older children.

My father took me to an eye specialist, who kindly assumed that I lived up to my name—at which my father answered the well-meaning doctor with frowning bitterness: "She did once!"

I can date my fall from grace to this instant.

To shed my previously assumed false role was a relief and eventually my salvation, but when it happened, the role was tied to the withered umbilical cord of parental love.

Parents cannot possibly realize what a traumatic experience it is to be catapulted from grace like that—even if they always appreciated you for the wrong reasons. The child loses confidence, starts playing different roles in confused desperation, trying to guess which behavior will assure maximum success.

One tries so hard at obedience, that in the end *somebody else,* "the bad Sun" wets the bed, pilfers in school, masturbates, vomits and, in moments of mad hidden rebellion, takes over "the good girl" and explodes in attacks of anger and hate that create fear in the parents and cause even more repressive, well-intentioned measures. When I was very young they appreciated the same things that they later blamed me for.

I was called "sunshine" because of my supposedly sunny and happy disposition. I was generous and conciliating, trying to spread sweetness and light between the warring factions in the family, between the parents, between parents and children and between everybody and myself. I laughed and made myself sweet and charming, sitting up like a good little doggy for rewards, sweets and love.

I knew that Mama loved all that was pretty. I chose my inherited finery with great care and tried to resemble Shirley Temple. Mama's German women friends found me irresistible and praised me for my good taste and my coquetry.

A few years later she reprimanded me severely for my *"Eitelkeit,"* my vanity. Now when I wanted to choose my dresses, I was beaten, torn to bits with threats and shouts by my already mentally disturbed mother. She lamented the fact that I did not strive for heaven "in order that everything should be mine" but that I insisted to be allowed to dress like an ordinary Swedish school girl instead of looking like a cross between a figure out of the Grimm fairy tales and Max und Moritz. I wore red hooded capes, crocheted multicoloured wool dresses looking like ball gowns, dresses made out of velvet curtains with square lace-collared necklines like a parody of Velázquez stuffed children. I had to wear lace-up boots, children's military style coats and hats from Germany.

My readiness to render services was now called ingratiation. If anybody wanted to console or support me, that was forbidden and called pampering. The same nice ladies who at one time had received me when Mama wanted me out of the way were now slandered, and I was forbidden to meet them "for my own sake."

When I laughed loudly, Papa was requested to beat me.

I must have been seven or eight years old, and I was laughing hysterically when my parents were having a dinner party. The children were dining in the kitchen, the older ones encouraging me to laugh more and more. I was willing to do anything to curry favor with them, and went on laughing, although Papa warned me repeatedly and finally gave me a good hiding. From sheer fright, I wet my pants and in the end I had to ask Papa's forgiveness for his willingness to beat me when Mama asked him to.

Even today, when I laugh loudly—and I do, frequently, like a "brewer's drayman," as they used to say at home—I feel a twinge of fear. I always apologize humbly and say, "Yes, isn't it awful the way I laugh like a real drayman."

Sibling love!

The structure of our family, *and our family was not exceptional,* was mercilessly puritanical and occasionally violent, the violence not openly showing but repressed. With the best of intentions, children were oppressed or "trained," but control over and within the family was used as a welcome and unconscious outlet for the parents' own aggressions for the indignities and injustices they had suffered. Anybody who has been controlled should be allowed to control others.

All this made its mark on the children. Playfulness and joy were tinged with cruelty. We played one off against the other, distributed orders and punishments. I developed my own line of defense against the older ones, used sweetness as a weapon: made myself irresistible, learned to charm. I had never known I possessed this resource, but it was useful when all other lines of defense were broken.

I mainly tried to charm my brothers, whom I loved and feared, playing them one against the other, unconsciously and relentlessly trying to disarm them.

One day the older was the best and my darling, the next day my only thought was for the younger.

It simply was not possible to defy or contradict them. They had to be approached from below, from the position of the slave. They were like Papa and had learned from him. They were big, strong and beautiful and knew how to handle and make use of women, and they found that sisters were useful to practice on. I was constantly running errands.

I remember that a large part of my childhood seemed to be spent running errands; if they could not invent sensible tasks, there would be meaningless or oppressing ones, in order to mask the pain they themselves felt as oppressed. Oppressor and oppressed. They had been running errands for their parents, that was part of the training; it "does not hurt to learn to work," but it lays the foundation for a neurotic need to dominate and intimidate others. It is a common need.

All these services and errands and other little attentions were only "for fun." It even amused me at times to notice how pliant and obliging I could be; but I had of course been practising on Papa in order to gain his love.

The more my brothers found me amusing and encouraged me, the more I tried to clown, using all my ingenuity playing for laughs, grimly comical. I made myself coarse, ugly, dressed up as and caricatured various people. I learned to imitate persons and was told that I was "destined to become an actress."

I worshipped my brothers, in spite of my fear or maybe because of it. They in their turn loved and protected me, and I found their occasional cruelty amply compensated for by the security they gave me.

As I grew older, I learned to see and love them as ordinary human beings, to see their uncertainty and despair, disappointments and anxiety. I forgot and "forgave" the cruel games so that I would be forgiven for the cruelty I was sure to commit one day.

All this I could not grasp at the time.

I did not understand that I had been conditioned by my father and brothers to love all men from below, kneeling with my neck bent, to hide shame, fury and defiance.

I offered them—and most men, from then on—with my neck obediently bent, a wide and humbly smiling mouth, a blood-red, sore mouth to be kissed and violated.

Figures of light

I used to escape from home when the going got rough, and that happened quite often. I ran away to "Solön," not far from our house, and climbed "my own tree," the higher up the better.

For a time I had a friend, Kent, as an anchor in my existence. He was my one and only friend, loyal unto death, my playmate from "Gården." I think many of us carry a "Kent" inside. The one who never failed us, who remains even if life has separated us, he who personifies reality, knowledge that not only misery and deceit exist but light as well, that goodness, even when hidden, is a force.

Kent was one year younger than I and, as I remember, blond, light-skinned, Swedish looking. He was the only son of Uncle Gustavsson, who worked at the plant breeding institute. Kent was meek and loyal, and though I might have had a chance to oppress him, I did not. I tended him like a precious plant. He had always wished for a brother and I pretended to be a brother, sharing his boyish games, talking in a deep voice, bold—as bold as he was. I knew how boys were; I had studied my own brothers. Kent and I were equals. I was included and accepted in the "Gården" collective of Bergstedt and Falkman, I was not a worthless child or the boss's daughter but a snotty brat and an inquisitive chatterbox, whom they liked just as they liked their own brats.

Snot, that was one big problem. It did not help much to inhale, there always seemed to be this greenish yellow gluey substance blocking the upper lip. Before the advent of Kleenex, one had to be lucky to get hold of bogpaper, and handkerchiefs were only for adult use or on the rather painful occasions when somebody big would grab one's nose and shout "Blow!"

Kent taught me to block one nostril at a time and blow out in the air. He was very clever at it and I practised until I learned the trick. One other, rather disgusting, method was to suck it into the mouth and then spit it out when nobody was watching. I very much admired Kent for his nose; he actually was able to inhale a piece of India rubber through the nose and spit it out.

We met every day after school—and before reaching school age we used to play all day. Mama did not consider Kent to be a suitable playmate, but she relented for the blessed relief not to have me underfoot all the time.

I hung around Kent's kitchen instead, where I was treated to solid Swedish food: herrings and spuds. No silly rules about table manners, like Mama's idea that stuffing one cheek was the polite thing to do.

Kent's mother was kind and understanding. If she worried about unsuitability, it was probably whether I was a good playmate for Kent. I was nervous, naughty and inventive, coaxing her delighted son into many scurvy tricks. He was as bold as I; not worse, just equal.

We had our private world and our private language. We created fantasy figures, generally mean and nasty—or rather, I invented and Kent approved. One of them was a statuesque invisible lady standing by Big Pond, selling poisoned shoe polish. Her name was Dajda and she was terrible to children so we had to invent different means of escaping her.

Mostly life for us was idyllic. We practised balancing on the garden seats and on the enormous wooden snow plough, which we used as our own private home and castle every autumn, spring and those summers we weren't farmed out at different summer camps. Half the plough served as a living room, the other half as a nursery.

My brothers ignored Kent and Kent did not admire them

for their superiority in age and size. He belonged to me and I to him. On the few occasions he came to my home he changed, and that frightened me. He used to stay in the doorway, bowing, cap in hand, shyly refusing to raise his eyes from the floor. "He can't be a good boy," Mama proclaimed, "he is surely hiding something. He never looks you in the eye." Just imagine if Kent had known what was hidden in Mama's eyes.

I could not wait to escape and pretended to eat meals at home, but hid the food instead before going home with Kent to eat fried bacon and potatoes. Kent's next-door neighbors had a nickname for me, "Beggarbrat." They were not friendly and hated everything to do with our family. Occasionally they gave me nuts and raisins and then they used their nickname for me. Their daughter disliked us to the extent that she later changed her surname for Mama's German maiden name, although spelled differently. I found life very puzzling.

When we were about eight years old I pulled down Kent's trousers and was allowed to look at him and in return he was allowed to look at me. Later he showed me some daring but gorgeous pages in a magazine he had found. The magazine was *Folket i Bild*, a genuine product of the common people, with contributors like Fridegård and Ahlin and others not as well known. They wrote about real life, and we read with glowing cheeks about unsophisticated people arriving in Stockholm, about girls getting into trouble in the hotbed of sin and also about sweaty love in the haystacks. Sweat, by the way, was not allowed in my home. Big, calloused and sweaty hands cupping round, firm breasts on a sofa in Söder. Söder was the traditional working class area of Stockholm.

Kent was already an accomplished lady-killer. Sometimes he brought girls home from his school, and on these occasions I thought he was too bold and forward when I stood, sulking by the snow plough, angry and jealous, daring them to go into "our" home. Kent did not play us girls against each other, rather the opposite. From my own school I was used to being excluded by the other children, whom I found frightening. I had tried to make friends with them, one after the other, and failed. Children neither want to nor do they dare to be friendly with somebody so obviously odd. Mama made me look like a clown, and that, together with the fact that she was a foreigner, made me an outsider.

It was not only that Mama was German, which was nothing less than a catastrophe during the war. But teachers, parents and children did not like any foreigners. Being half foreign, I know what it is to be isolated, an outsider in Sweden, and I have never felt at home in a collective outside Slottsskogen. I only had Kent and Auntie Rill and Gården, and Kent let me have a taste of the joy of playing with children who genuinely and spontaneously showed that they liked me and wanted to play with me.

I soon made friends with the girls Kent brought; they knew nothing of Mama and I forgot to sulk. It helped that I was allowed to wear ordinary rough clothes for play. This made me look like the others.

Kent never found me odd, strangely enough. He knew and liked me from the inside and did not mind how I looked.

As with nature, if you really know it and love it, you do not look at it from the outside. You use it for living, playing, climbing the trees, breathing the sweet air; there is no need to make it into an artificial paradise—into art.

Kent's father suddenly fell ill. In a routine screening, he was found to be in the terminal stages of tuberculosis. Unlike mama, he was not treated at a private sanatorium; he was spared visions of dying seamen, he knew nothing of writing poety or painting. No solemn men in white coats bothered to stop by his bedside to talk to him. He was not given any treatment in time, and his condition had been aggravated by living in a cold and drafty house.

Kent's father died the death of a Swedish working man, with speed and without fuss. The funeral was simple and ghostly. Kent changed; pork and potatoes never tasted the same in their kitchen again. His mother was wrapped in dark sadness, in the aura of her dead husband, and she was weighed down with anxiety. Kent and I drifted apart; we were older and by now familiar with illness and death.

Between us stood a coffin and a definable darkness.

The memory of feeling often works in such a way that you remember the surroundings of the beloved person: her tables and chairs, her white bread rolls, her coat, her way of walking.

I cannot remember the whole Auntie Rill; I was too young to look at her other than as part of myself and my feelings for her. I understood her intuitively—not consciously.

She lived in a forester's lodge near the edge of Slottsskogen, close to Big Pond. She had been secretary to my father but was by now retired. She was alone, unmarried, without relatives in Gothenburg, very rarely visited by an uncle from Värmland. For many years she had been an intimate friend of the family and I knew that Mama liked her very much until the time came when anybody could arbitrarily find or lose favor with Mama. In Auntie Rill's case, it was undeserved animosity, directed against the first really good person I had ever known intimately. Her whole person was mildness, everything rounded, polished, soft and understanding, her life relaxed and at the same time quietly waiting on events, nothing remotely frightening about her.

I became her little "golden hen," and I liked to be a Swedish golden hen as a change from "ein Lieblingskind," a well-intentioned endearment—but German.

I did not find her old. She was, like Kent, a contemporary. Very old people and small children can become close friends, possibly because the child has not learned to pretend and toil—and the old person has tired of pretense and toil. I had only just appeared out of darkness and eternity and she was soon going back, and for a short while we were friends.

Autie Rill had known me since birth and she had often

helped my tired Mama with her last little bundle. I often visited the little cottage in the woods, and she herself and her life became part of the stories she told me. These stories were not German and not unreal but described her own childhood and adolescence in Värmland, and every story was full of meaning and importance to a child.

Story time over, we would go to the kitchen where she cooked potatoes with syrup and baked white bread, the like of which I have never ever tasted. She was poor and the bread had only simple, plain ingredients; flour, water, yeast—or was it maybe some herb that made it taste like heaven? We split the warm bread and buttered it and opened the basket with cheese and sausage that I had carried through the forest from Mama. No wolf had eaten Auntie Rill and no witch was waiting for Gretel, only a playmate who always had time to spare. The cottage and everything in it was tiny, and I loved that. Two little old ladies or two small children sitting and talking about the deep forests of Värmland, about wolves and bears, about "the girl who used bread as stepping-stones"; and afterwards we ate the bread, which nobody would dream of stepping on, only revere and respect.

She and Papa had similar experiences of poverty, but she did not admonish. I was spared the preaching, just as she was spared the task of educating and could be nothing but "kind."

She knew which stories could comfort, like the following: Once upon a time there was a little girl called Gunhild, who lived with her parents in a poky little cottage. Upstairs lived a lonely old lady called Auntie Ester. Gunhild possessed only one good dress to be used only on special occasions. For school she dressed in everyday clothes. In school there was a mean girl called Britta, who always teased Gunhild for wearing the cast-off clothes from the daughters of the minister. Britta's mother was a seamstress and Britta was always well dressed but not a clever or nice girl. Gunhild got tired of listening to the stuck-up Britta and one day, when her mother was not looking, she dressed in her fine green dress.

Her friends in school admired her nice dress but the jealous Britta spattered her with mud on the way home. This was a terrible thing to happen and Gunhild cried and cried. She was going to a party the same night and her mother was sure to find out and scold her and probably beat her. What to do? She thought of Auntie Ester, who was kind and lonely, and she decided she would tiptoe upstairs and try to enlist Auntie's help, but quietly so that her mother would not notice.

She ran all the way home, slipped upstairs, listened at the door, knocked, and when Auntie Ester opened it, fell into her arms crying.

"Yes, good advice is at a premium," said Auntie Ester. "Let's wash it at once and then I will iron it and hang it up to dry in front of the fire. Meanwhile I will go downstairs and fetch one of your other dresses. But remember in the future that lying is evil and let this be a lesson for you not to listen to that silly Britta when she teases you about your plain clothes. Poverty is not shameful."

Saying this, she fetched another dress, and washed and ironed the green one until it looked as good as new. Now they heard somebody coming up the stairs and mother's voice calling, "Ester, is Gunhild with you?"

And there was the dress hanging, for all to see! "Come in, my dear," said Auntie. "Gunhild just now came to show me her nice dress she will be wearing tonight, and I ironed it for her." Mother grumbled: "I don't know what gets into the girl. She is always hanging about up here with you and I am afraid that you spoil her. How will I teach her to behave?"

"Ah, well," said Auntie, "I also try to do my bit, but clay should be shaped with soft hands."

"What did she mean?" I always used to ask. "You will understand one day," Auntie Rill always answered, adding: "Nobody caresses a cat with a clenched fist."

Auntie Rill was the first who took me downtown to Gothenburg, and as we had all the time in the world, we proceeded in a leisurely fashion. We strolled down to the park gates and bought ice cream. After that we boarded a tram that went in a circle through the whole town, across the new bridge by the harbor to Hisingen, where there was a fine view of the sea and all the big ships and back again, across Lilla Bommen to Slottsskogen. Auntie Rill soon fell asleep, her beautiful face falling in gentle folds, shaking with the movement of the tram. Now and again she would open one large fold, and another smaller fold, and from deep within, a sleepy eye peered out to see if I was enjoying myself—as indeed I was, dreaming of the sea and the ships and those foreign shores she had been telling me about. When we thundered across the bridge, I found that her stories were real, the beautiful and mighty sea was there, just as she had said, and my whole being was filled with indescribable happiness. I was very young—much too young really to long intensely for other than everyday things.

Opposite my longing sat the old queen of fairy tales with silver hair like spun sugar round her loving face, and on top of the silver sat a serene black hat from Värmland, keeping us both in order.

Our pace when we walked round Slottsskogen was even slower. She had to stop, out of breath, and admire the view we had seen hundreds of times. "Look, how lovely the world is." She did not have the strength to walk with me uphill and we stayed most of the time in her little cottage. She seemed to revert to a second childhood, and that suited me fine, but she kept falling asleep and she never again baked the white bread.

Her strength failed and in the end they had to take her away. I had nowhere to go and the entire forest collapsed from sorrow.

I saw her in hospital, when her heart barely had the strength to beat, one tired beat at a time, one lonely life and one beat for each fantasy and each fairy story, two beats for reality and four for dreams. Auntie Rill, who knew that only soft hands can make beautiful pots out of clay, lay there strangely far away in Värmland, in a sleigh lined with fur against the cold, with howling wolves chasing after the horses and after the sleigh and after her, and the wolves were going to catch up with her, she who was so good, and the cold would overtake her, she who had been so full of warmth.

The wolves of death would vanquish the tender green life and the open sea. It was not fair.

Not fair to anybody.

Dear beloved Mama

By now I have written many pages about my childhood and about you and about my failure to become reconciled to you. I have sometimes felt like a slanderer—when I have told of my black memories and of my fear of the adult world.

When I have been writing about you, it has happened that I have risen in the middle of night to bar my door, afraid of your revenge, but all that is in the past. Now I can finally describe my longing and my understanding and my memories of the good mother.

You were not the only person in the world to give vent to violent feelings, to fatigue and illness, not alone in bitterness and disappointment. Millions of women have been forced to suffer from bad conscience for failing to be good and patient mothers and millions have broken under the strain of having to please, of having to act the expected roles, frustrated in their efforts to realize their full potential.

You had to endure monotonous hard labor and take care of four children, you had to be the home economist and solve all the domestic problems, and you had to pinch and save to make ends meet.

Your husband demanded a captivating, tender and understanding wife, who could charm in the social sense while remaining a serious and faithful believer, strict and morally irreproachable. You were not allowed to be carefree and bohemian—something you always longed for. You were rarely allowed to satisfy artistic and creative needs. Sick with guilt, you had to steal the time to write or paint.

You went to the beach to paint the sea and your tired, shaking hands knocked the easel over in the sand, with the painting almost completed.

You often cried bitterly over the loss of creative life.

Everything you had been taught in Germany as being an unquestionable right was suddenly considered wrong, criminal, despised.

It must have been difficult to meet so much hate in a foreign country. Your countrymen and brothers were called executioners and murderers. Everything had turned out wrong and you alone could not put it right.

For years and years you simply could not understand what was happening, and when you finally did understand—you died.

I remember the softness of your embrace that gave me all the comfort in the world.

I remember your fairy tales and how you taught me to dream in the dark.

I remember your warmth and your imagination. You did understand much that concerned your children, but moral obstacles would sometimes collide with your sympathy and understanding and make you withhold your love.

I remember your love as sudden attention, when you would scoop me up and talk to me as if I were grown up.

You used to invite our friends and bestow kisses on their cheeks, in a very un-Swedish manner that they at first found odd and ended up loving you for.

You gave presents to one and all, and you knew instinctively what to give. You invited complete strangers to share our meals and there was always a place at the table "for the unknown guest."

Your generosity made us poor in one sense but very rich in another.

During the war the house was filled to capacity.

Your kitchen curtains were so tattered that the workmen in the forest gave you new ones, and in return you invited them to drink the brandy that, I think, Papa had been given as a present for helping somebody design a garden. With the brandy you talked to them about socialism and Jesus. They loved you and forgot very soon that you came from Germany.

That time when you had broken a leg, you managed to get around on your bicycle with your leg in an enormous plaster cast, dressed in a long strange-looking coat and a large picture hat with feathers and plumes. Everybody you met laughed at you and you smiled sweetly in return. You treated them to a free show, a one-woman comic opera performance.

You knew many amusing games and you taught us to play in solitude and like it. You built a puppet theatre with puppets and acted all the parts in the show with enormous success. You believed in simplicity and goodness of the soul and had the naiveté of a child. People were known to speculate on how you had managed to conceive four children.

Once a year you arranged a party for the children and we had a game called "Begegnen" in which couples went round the house asking those they met whether he or she chose "pear" or "apple."

This was the most daring game in your repertoire and you never stopped giggling.

At Easter you told us you were a German Easter bunny and that we had to find the marzipan you had hidden in the forest. It very often ended with you consoling your weeping children who could not find the marzipan, and by this time you too had forgotten where it was hidden.

You were an unsurpassed teller of ghost stories, the same stories that had frightened you as a child and that you believed as gospel.

You blessed our sandwiches before we went for our written exams and you always sided with us against our teachers.

You loved animals and could not understand why Papa wanted to kill them.

You came to school, sat at the back of the classroom and whispered to those who were stuck for an answer.

You brought sweets for everybody at school when you came.

You hugged me so hard that heaven fell down and we had some trouble getting untangled from the clouds and finding our way back to earth.

You met me sometimes in the forest on my way back from

school and you talked to me as if I were the only person you loved in the whole wide world.

You spoiled me on the few occasions you had the time and strength to be with me.

We were conspirators going to a delicatessen while the older children were at school, or to Brautigam's tearoom for ice cream, and we were both totally happy for a couple of hours in the world.

You hurried home from a party once when we had been left alone, because you felt that something threatened us, and you found a burglar in the bushes, about to break into the house.

You could tell fortunes in molten tin and in palms.

Homosexual men loved you and never left you in peace, bringing you their problems.

You "took the cancer" from an old actress who came to you for help and when you picked it up yourself, you thought you were Jesus.

You looked after Finnish war invalids and Russian immigrant workers, inviting them for dinner, even to share our Christmas.

You did everything spontaneously. You did not knit socks for soldiers at the front in order to feel excellent—you were not very good at either sewing or knitting; all your efforts in that direction usually turned into disasters.

Like the Greeks do, you liked to feed everybody at the table to show them how much you loved them.

You cared too much about people and you were apt to swamp them with sympathy. Your moral sense tended to get in the way like a truncheon hitting you over the head.

You fell in love, platonically, with the doctors who treated you and sometimes with friends, passing by.

You insisted that the little people, who lived under the leaves, were benevolent.

You wanted to meet me every day but rarely found the time, and I ran and cried and looked for you and cried and ran all the way from school for too many years of my life.

You let me walk home on my own in the winter darkness after

my dancing lessons and you vowed that nothing could happen to me because you had blessed the forest. You had blessed the forest!

You gave everything away, including the shirt off your back, if nobody stopped you.

You used to laugh until you fell over. If you started crying you could go on for ever. Your quarrels could last a year.

You did not know Papa and were eternally surprised to see him in your bed.

You thought the body was useful for two things only: household chores and breast-feeding.

You believed in raw vegetables and thought that carrots would cure you. Later on you believed in garlic and later still in the ashes from a fakir.

You held conversations with your dead and often predicted death.

You hid in your illness as in an untimely crucifixion, hoping for resurrection and for a life after death.

As soon as you left a room, it felt empty.

Nobody could be more alive than you.

I must be allowed to speak freely, for once, to enjoy absolute freedom when I write, without feeling the hard school desk in my back. I want to write exactly how I feel and still dare to hope that what I write will be received—openly and with understanding.

All my life I have had to sit through lessons and, against my will, admit to fear of the teachers.

Of the critics.

Of the authorities.

"Is it really permissible to write like that?"

But wait! Wait for a few years and I will be a changed person. Then I will have read all the books that are a must. All the books that everybody says one simply must have read to be considered an educated person. Wait a few days, months and years until the day comes when I have suppressed myself and my inner needs. Then I will be to my sisters and brothers as they want me to be. Then they will want my books, my articles and my views.

Wait until I have succeeded in obliterating myself.

Wait until I have learned to please everybody. Not too individual but enough. Not too erudite but learned enough. Not too stiflingly feminine but Woman through and through. Liberated and conscious of my sex but not a man hater.

Critical toward tradition and toward present-day values.

Critical toward dreamers as well as toward academics and worshippers of reason.

Independent in relation to the left and the right, in relation to critics—but humble, sensitive and open to "what is going on at the time."

Sensitive and insensitive.

"Can this be of any possible interest to anybody but herself and her immediate family?"

Men generally fear the personal, that impenetrable jungle, so take care!

Also—take care not to pander to women's interest in the personal, unless this interest can be lifted out of the area of gossip.

The too personal is considered pornographic when it concerns a separate saleable part of the body or the soul, dressed up for scandal or sensation.

What is then so dangerous when a woman is personal and writes about herself? Is her openness a threat? Is there a risk that the Oppression is about to be revealed at last?

I long to read a male author who dares to be completely personal and open and honest about all of his life.

Why does this suddenly stop me in my tracks? Is it because this ought to be written in another context or in another book?

I hear stern voices berating me. Do I dare? Am I allowed? But this cannot be considered particularly daring or couragous. I am desperate!

Could I be right in feeling or imagining—that a majority *does not want* me to write?

They do and they don't want it, they are jealous and rejoice simultaneously. Everybody wants to write, get out of stifling anonymity and be recognized. Well, go on, write! Write the way you think and talk. Now, when almost nobody dares to live or meet others, when you cannot meet people for lack of meetingplaces. An infamously deliberate set of limitations that stops you and me from uniting and thereby strengthening ourselves—against what? Against destructive authorities.

One admires male authors, who are not too personal, and when they write in contrast to prevailing styles their audacity is praised to the skies.

They are wonderful and remarkable, but not because they hide, with the help of cathedrals of jewels and junk, built to obstruct their identity and private problems—but because they involuntarily, in spite of all the smoke screens, show themselves, startled and disguised, through their walls and labyrinths.

Joyce and Beckett are admired for their literary style more than for their message.

The personal must not *appear* as personal. But the personal must be what refers to a person, why then make it so very difficult?

One reason could be that bourgeois society is doing very well, thanks to the high walls that include only equals, where outsiders are not admitted.

Or is it that we are a heterogeneous multitude, where nobody dares to draw attention to his own nose for fear of being singled out as different and abnormal? Maybe there is a longing to find *one* formula to contain everything that is human, where all the mysteries can be collected in one sum total. But if that were possible, it would be equally possible to manufacture gold, and the alchemists have, so far, failed in that task.

It cannot be possible to know about others before knowing and daring to talk about oneself.

The carrot is interesting only when it is out of the earth, even if the green on top can give pleasure.

In fiction, for various known reasons mostly created by men, the qualities, good and bad, real and imagined, are projected onto invented characters, who serve as spokesmen for oneself. Different qualities are often divided between several fictional characters or can be, at best, accommodated in one single person, called Arvid instead of August. This is of great advantage— not least for moralists.

This way one avoids being called "personal," avoids the pain of recognition and the necessity to take a stand against intrusive problems, sticky problems. One does not have to pocket the ignominy.

One has learned one's lessons at school and at university and one knows how to present them in their wrappings of eternal thought. One claims to look for the truth when one cannot or refuses to look into oneself.

If something of oneself should turn up, it is easy to hide behind the tree of knowledge. Words and ideas embraced by many for millennia, whether right or wrong, are worshipped because they allow for escape from one's own deprived, tiresome and lost self, but their structure often feels strange and unreal because of the mass of ideas that has molded us human beings into others than we were, that has enclosed the living body in armor, that has forced us to become what we were not intended to be.

To be oneself is to be like the others.

One's own life is always valid for others and vice versa.

We have too much in common to be allowed to escape.

November is here and darkness is welling forth—thicker each day. I can even smell the dark and the decay and the approaching cold. Nothing can warm me. I light innumerable fires, pile on clothes, but I feel the cold all the time—from within.

I find people around me colder than they were in September.

Friends come visiting to Victoria and I try to fire myself and them into a glow—with food and wine, but the warmth does not last. When they leave, it turns even more still and cold, they seem to drain the supplies left by summer and beautiful autumn to leave more room for the onslaught of winter. How can we stand winter year after year? This perpetual death.

For years I used to spend this season in a cheap boarding house on the Danish coast. Darkness seems less thick by the sea, water can switch off the dark just as it can put out a fire. The sound of the waves creates a feeling of continuity. Everything is repeated and returned. We will return, you and I.

It is not easy to write in darkness and cold. One turns down the flame and crouches and hides one's thoughts so as not to disturb the other guests at the funeral. Do not shout or you wake death, only death will come anyway.

Last night I dreamed of P whom I have not seen in twelve years. He was ill when I saw him last and in my dream he was dying. I visited him in hospital and found him contented and happy and alive within his illness. He was in high spirits and seemed glad to see me—but wanted me to leave almost immediately. He turned his face to the wall and continued to ingratiate himself with death, as if death and he had already formed a delightful and profitable relationship and only the last remained—to surrender his body to the nurses. His face had a warm rosy color and he seemed elated, even animated, in what seemed to me an almost indecent way.

I went away, feeling far sadder than my dying friend. Death seemed to exist within *me*, as rigid and cold and merciless as it had been described in books.

I mourned, not my friend, but the withheld farewell and the sharp borderline between him, sentenced to death and oblivion, and myself, still alive and possibly with a future.

It did not make me feel more alive. Nobody gains by another's death.

I had never seen anybody dying before I had to witness my mother's incredibly violent death. She died in Papa's arms after suffering two massive hemorrhages. In the general confusion, I had to watch the whole drama together with the older children, because we had been herded together to stand united.

It was too dramatic to be immediately horrible. We were witnessing a wrestling match between Life and Death. My mother fought like a lioness although her body was emaciated and she had very little strength left—but what little she had, she used in her last fight.

In the first round she was held upright while the blood poured into a bucket at her feet, later she became unconscious and lay on the bed in her spotted red and white nightgown, that kept riding up over the knees. She kicked off the blankets, the gown kept riding up and she threw herself restlessly this way and that, as if she were having a nightmare or maybe a fit of nerves before the final bout.

The sight was too affecting for anybody to be merely a spectator, and I somehow entered her and fought with her.

Ever since my birth I had tried to live inside her because that was what she wanted, at first. Later when she decided to push me away, it was perhaps because she realized that I was too firmly and dangerously tied to her. Closeness like that can be compared to the state of the unborn child staying in the womb for years, too long, threatening life.

The second round started toward evening. I don't think she was fully awake when the blood started pouring through nose and mouth, but she gave the impression of being wide awake and fighting—like a maniac—for her life.

By this time I had slipped into an unreal state of mind, without conscious effort and without pain. I only felt deep compassion with somebody weak, being attacked by a brutal and disgusting giant and I could do nothing to help, only watch.

Mama hung between Papa and the nurse, helpless like a small child or the victim of a traffic accident, surprised by mortal and undeserved injuries. This was the epitome of something vitally important and at the same time gratingly futile. You would never dare to build your life on either of the two extremes, the futility of death or belief in its significance.

Death is always a surprise, a new experience, concerning nobody but yourself. It is of no importance if you are a thousand times reconciled to death or if you firmly believe that heaven is waiting in the hereafter. Anything is possible but there is only one certainty. Death is going to devastate your brain and your flesh, break your heart, set your eyes looking in surprise out toward the well-known and inward to the unknown. The smile changes to a grimace, the grimace to a smile. A clenched hand does not open and the open hand can only be closed with force.

Painless childbirth is not without physical sensations, and I think that even painless death, however much prepared for through life-long exercises, is thoroughly experienced in body and soul.

I remember how she tossed her head from side to side, how her arms were beating the air, how she tried to draw breath through the streams of blood pouring forth. I stood quite close to her when her eyes rolled upward and I realized then that it was the end. I left her bed, rushed downstairs and knelt against a chair, trying desperately to concentrate on what was playing on the wireless. I prayed to God that he should help her to die, up there in her room, and I had the sensation, even stronger than before, that I was my mother, that I would be forced to live her life or that her life forever had taken possession of me.

I had seen everything happen but was protected from the impact by a drugged feeling, cocooned in my own soft and misty world.

The feeling of pain came later, to stay for a very long time.

The physical death in itself that I had witnessed was not what was going to fill me with deep anxiety and unease of spirit for many years to come. That particular death was a vivid reminder of life.

The blood was red and warm. The body moved and fought and wailed. It was a concentration of life among spectators who seemed less alive, the color of red seemed to cover us, flowed like a magnificent cloak on the floor by her chalk-white feet. Her white nightgown was given a resplendent rose, that grew until it covered the whole garment. In the heat of the struggle, her hair floated in black and grey clouds across her narrow shoulders and every muscle, every nuance of face and body seemed to participate. The scene, as I remember it, had the same naked and unreserved quality as the act of making love. Dying or making love, you have no defenses.

The body always speaks the truth, while thinking means lying; it is as simple and fundamental as the growth of an ear of corn. Pain and suffering are undisguised in the face of death. The departure from life is our last reality, the truth we can trust blindly. Dying is not ugly.

Death is neither ugly nor beautiful, neither poetry nor work of art. It is self-evident but incomprehensible and impenetrable by nature.

You must disappear after having lived and learned and made mistakes in order to become dust and ashes.

Emptiness fills your chair and silence takes your place at the table. An ingenious futility that has made us speculate during thousands of years.

Death has not frightened me since that day—but rather the absence of red pulsating blood, of heartbeats, of life.

A physician once said to me what might appear self-evident, but I understand his bleak statement: There is nothing more dead than a corpse.

A cold, colorless, stiff and unprotesting body. A body that *once possessed* life—the absence of life underlines the definitive, conclusive emptiness, like the bag emptied of Christmas presents or the clock-work bear with its spring broken. When the corpse has been washed and laid out, it resembles a wax doll.

There is a custom, in Greece, to dress up and embellish the corpse, as if to soften the obscene impression of a friend to whom one chatted in the morning and who decided to slip away around noon without much ado. A friend, who stepped out of his body and was gone in a few seconds. This vanishing act is treacherous, infamous and frightening, especially to those who had trusted their friend for his firm reality. They had always relied on his helpfulness and his ability to listen or on his mocking, provoking comments or on his irritating habit of picking his nose openly, even in elegant company.

One feels suddenly deprived, robbed, betrayed.

When my own mother lay there, dead and changed, it was this corpse—the dead body that had once been alive—that was going to frighten me for many years to come. She appeared in nightmares, in waking fantasies where I often met a waxy apparition, a ghost, an undelivered sorrow, a living horror that I had to carry with me always. Her poor corpse had to carry every negative experience, imagined or real, that I was forced to live through but was reluctant to face up to. All my pain had found its symbolic habitation in my dead mother's ghost, haunting me year after year.

In the light of day I could remember my good, creative and happy mother, but I was anxiously looking over my shoulder while I forced myself to project her saintly and ethereal qualities. At night, she came to haunt me, even while I was still awake. She would come stealthily in the dark, her face bloated and yellow, and lean over me, hissing "It was you who gave me the cancer." "*Du warst ja immer ungehorsam.*"

Beside myself with fear, I used to scream night after night until Papa lost his patience. After that I shut up but started shaking instead.

It was not unusual for me to meet people in Slottsskogen who looked like Mama at a distance. My terror increased as this person approached with her coat, her hair and her face. When we were finally face to face, there was always the same waxen image staring at me with a mixture of accusion and self-absorbed sorrow. "*Du hast mich getötet.*" "You have killed me."

It is quite true, I had wished her dead. We all ended up wishing for her death by the time she had suffered from her incurable disease during two or three years, without hope for a remedy. It would take the cancer four years to quench life in her. That was one reason Mama believed that her illness was punishment for her sins. The doses of morphine were not sufficient to ease the pain when the cancer had invaded her entire nervous system. Yes, we wished for her death, I wished for it so intensely that I used to dream, after she was dead, that she was still alive and in the dream I would make my wish come true. We all longed for a release from the heartrending moans and the suffering and, most of all, from this interminable leave-taking. It seemed as if we were sharing our home with an unburied corpse and this corpse was wont to accuse one or the other of us with murder and treason. We had to watch while the fine mechanism and intricate clockwork of her brain collapsed into disparate parts indicating the wrong time, the wrong year, the wrong life.

As a special favor to her daughters, which she expected us to appreciate, Mama had promised to materialize after her death. She had predicted that it would take her soul seven years to break loose from the grip of death.

During seven years I was haunted by Mama's waxy yellow face. When I think about it now, I cannot understand why she never showed herself in another guise. Why did I always have to see her as this frightening apparition? Even in my sleep I smelled the stench from her putrefying body. During the first seven years after Mama's death, I fought to keep her memory away, day and night. I tried to obliterate her face, tensing my body to stop her invading it. I was tense to the point of shaking for many years and it still happens, occasionally, that I wake up, shaking like an epileptic, with chattering teeth.

The nightmares disappeared, as promised, after seven years, even if the traces they left behind will remain with me always—however many books I write to exorcise them.

Almost exactly seven years to the day after Mama's death, I have this dream.

The location is Grahlsburg, a place I had only visited once, immediately before the outbreak of war in 1939. A group of formally dressed people talk quietly in a large room with thick carpets that muffle all sounds. There is anticipation in the air, something serious and important is about to happen. A staircase, also thickly carpeted, leads to the first floor and something unknown, waiting upstairs, is the cause of the excitement. I am standing, lonely and afraid, at the foot of the stairs when my sister appears. She whispers, gently and reassuringly, that she will come with me halfway up but after that I shall have to walk alone. I feel compelled to go, cautiously groping my way after my sister has left me, encouraging me to continue. She smiles and gestures, as if she knows what is going to happen—but this does not remove my fear.

I slip quietly up the remaining steps and enter a large room that resembles our drawing room at home. There is a fire in the fireplace, the room is in twilight, warm and cosy. I recognize the furniture, everything in its right place. There is the green sofa and in it, my mother. She is tiny, no more than three feet high. She is wearing her mauve velvet dressing gown and her dark hair rests on the velvet in a heavy plait. She looks the way she used to before she fell ill, but in miniature, small as a child or a dwarf as if she were afraid to frighten me with size.

She asks me to sit down beside her with a smile on her loving face that warms my whole body and I throw myself into her open arms, completely overcome. While I am in her arms, she starts growing, she is again big and soft and warm, she is my own good ordinary Mama. With a feeling of great relief, I start crying. She says, "All is well. You have nothing to fear anymore."

From then onward Mama has never appeared in my dreams other than as a figure of goodness and light. Sorrow and despair have found their own relief.

It occurs to me how difficult it is to be both honest and spontaneous as a writer. One must not exaggerate one's faults (thereby making them into virtues) or one's own suffering. One must not ooze fellow-feeling or brag with acquired wisdom.

One has to learn to listen to *one's own* voice and try to forget the wish to impress "the outside world." One reaches those outside best by letting them listen to one's true voice, whether it is happy or grumpy, angry or pathetic. A writer can seldom sustain one mood through three hundred and fifty pages.

I remember Louis Ferdinand Céline's novel *Journey to the End of the Night*. His vision is often black and the opinions he came to espouse may be wrong and objectionable, but in this book he is in harmony with himself.

He listens attentively to Louis Ferdinand Céline and he writes the way he talks, absolutely straight, concealing almost nothing of himself, neither embellishing nor distorting. His eyes have become used to the horrors of war, firmly rooted there, and he penetrates ever deeper into man's dark heart. He never uses the intricate, interesting but taxing technique that has operatic choirs, subconsciously and consciously singing away in a grandiose but untrained way: a bombardment of chaotic voices thrown at you as when a turbulent sea spits out her dead fishes or when shoals of fish ripple the surface of the water without giving you any idea of conditions of life and death and dreams, goals and disloyalties. Under these circumstances, you, the reader, are left floating, half-drowned on a primitive raft of your own making amidst the wreckage of a vast, mythical ship.

Céline, as human being and writer, is firmly anchored in life like anybody whose feet have been caught in a death-trap. The rest of the body makes frantic efforts to account for the experience and for the sensation to be alive against all odds.

I experienced *Journey to the End of the Night* as a liberation, mainly because Céline lacks the bragging and heroic superego which either is completely blind to the fact that there is a corpse in the cellar or, at the other extreme, deals "scientifically" with the same corpse with a fixed purpose of mind.

Céline has died and risen from the dead. He has had to confront the expected image of himself as man and professional medical man. He has recoiled in horror at the picture of himself and others in the novel. And then... he attempts to tell, without any illusions but with intense and piercingly bitter insight, alive and therefore positive—he attempts to shout loudly about life, he, Céline, doctor to the poor and madman.

I was thirteen years old. Mama was dead and the rest of the family seemed to be absent. All my energy was concentrated on growing up—and the effort to cope with the visions of horror and memories of hell I had been forced to live through in the past year.

I had nobody to talk to and that started me writing poetry. The others were busy with their own thoughts and their own survival.

One of my poems dedicated to mama:

> Lay your hand on my heart
> measure its sorrowful beats
> is it your wish that I live, half myself
> half another.
> Take me to you before all is bitter and black
> gather me up in your arms
> but soon—
> before I have mutely learned to endure.

I collected my poems and had them bound in a volume, handprinted by a friend to make it look like a real printed book. I dedicated the collection to my oldest brother and called it "A Handful of Leaves." The book has disappeared and that is just as well. Nostalgia has ever been a threat to my sense of reality.

Until the age of thirteen I never thought much about being a girl. During mama's long illness and even before that I felt closest to my brothers, and to Kent, of course. I was never made to feel inferior in matters like climbing trees, running, jumping and swearing like a trooper. I was fearless and could jump from higher diving-boards than my sister before I even knew how to swim. I was the youngest and most daring on the ski slopes—and on skates.

There were no prizes for guessing who had the most fun in this world, boys or girls. I did not even have to make a special effort, I was accepted as a matter of course, strangely enough. My brothers certainly never tried to encourage feminine behavior, rather the opposite. I had already dimly perceived how hellish it must be to give birth to one child after the other and to lack the strength to cope with them.

Later I tried to formulate the identity that exists in all women, free from sex definition. The right to be recognized as a thinking, free and independent being which presupposes being a socially and morally important part of humanity—outside the role of mother.

My sister had been thoroughly instructed in the feminine arts and in the role of wife and mother. She rapidly produced four children and would in all probability be at it still had she not been stopped, not from free will or desire but from a sense of duty, unconsciously fulfilling parental expectations.

My brothers were unwilling to think of me as a woman. That would only have complicated matters. We were very close, the three of us, while our sister was forced to accept a heavy, serious, caring and responsible role. All this was grossly unfair to her but no fault of ours.

My budding breasts surprised and alarmed them; later their teasing made me suddenly aware of my expanding forms. Mole-hills showing up under the jumper were pointed at and discussed at length. With me, everything seemed to bulge. My thighs, oh dear yes, my thighs! After six years of ballet practice, cycling, skating and skiing and then all those muscles covered with soft flesh, the result was worryingly feminine. Hips, thighs, bottom. Above the waist I remained fairly small—as an apology. I was allowed to dress like a boy, until my stepmother entered the lists and started dressing me like a lady. I refused at first to go along but accepted eventually, secretly pleased to step across the border and become a girl, to be allowed to play with boys on several levels, to test my power of attraction and to dream of love, all the things that older girls constantly and endlessly talked about. The transition from tomboy to girl took a long time and there still exists within me a double identity.

In my teens I used to wake up in the middle of the night, shaking, and Papa could not understand what was happening—it was not only the anxiety about Mama—no, I had a feeling of loss and alarm because I could not find the boy within me. I was no longer allied to the serene male world, where you belonged without effort and where, by virtue of your sex, you could cry "open Sesame" and expect to be given a large part of the splendor of the earth.

To be a woman implied having to fight. I witnessed Mama's tough battle to be allowed time and means and strength to reach the final goal, a human identity card.

Look, after hundreds of years of faithful service and many strenuous ordeals I have finally passed my existence examination. Am I now a member of the world? Am I allowed to express opinions and think and exert influence? It has been a long struggle.

I am a punching bag, heavily marked by all the fighting and the undeserved knockouts I have had to take.

I realize that men also face many struggles. I have lived with men all my life, closely within them. I observed my brothers and their sexual development, how they suffered insecurity and pain when they had to conquer their first girls. "Conquer" was the word. In the forties, boys worried a lot about their appearance. The tie had to be just so, the haircut likewise. They had to be good on the dance floor and not tread on toes, their hands must not be sweaty. If they felt romantic toward a girl, the erection had to be kept in check during the dance, and trembling hands were a bad sign. They had to stand up to their fellow competitors at school dances and then suddenly take a step into the male world, bragging about the willingness and submission of their victims. I was in a position to watch and listen to males from an early age. Ashen-faced teenagers who had been given the *coup de grace* by girlfriends and who were not allowed to cry. They were expected to drink, manfully and boldly—but not to the point of drunken vomiting.

Boys who blamed their own insecurity in bed on the girl's passivity: "She just lies there like some bloody mattress." I learned to interpret all this talk and understand that the meaning behind the words was not always bad, but insight like this is mind-blowing to a girl. Society expects men to fill their male roles, and in order to do that men are forced to hold back their understanding of women. Men have to be potent, secure, logical, masterful, strong, matter-of-fact, unsentimental, self-controlled . . .

I used to think about these things when I was very young and predict that it would take hundreds of years before men realized that their strength and power would not increase if they kept deadening a nerve and cutting off their understanding of women. Rather the reverse.

I always knew that too many sensitive and submissive women are the innocent victims of men's self-imposed blindness and regimented emotional life.

The female role is dangerously insecure and I was slowly adapting to it. I seemed to know that there was insecurity in store for me, because security implies full realization of human potential.

I gloomily realized that my attraction to men, as human beings and as sexual objects, meant that I had to accept female duties: cooking, caring, motherly comforts and the soft pliancy that does not provoke aggression. I have on occasion resisted the traditional role, at great cost to myself. I have had incredible invective thrown in my face when I have dared to oppose the male decree: inexplicable and hateful words said and shouted and howled at me.

As long as I was younger and more beautiful, a possible quarry and a gifted would-be partner, I was met by benevolent indulgence and generosity. One was quite willing to assist the woman-child, to admit that she was clever and to give one's male support to the cause of women's liberation. I am sorry to say that I aided and abetted my male superiors in their somewhat lukewarm support by being as accommodating as possible. I did not "hurt" them by being obstinate, and I kept my own writing and thinking and fighting in the background. As long as I was discreet, preferably invisible, I had their blessing.

When I grew older and could no longer fight against my anger in states of depression and crisis—then I was met by a frightening aggression or an icy wall of contempt.

"What is the matter with you?" somebody asked me once. "Are you trying to deny that you are a woman? You are fitted with a crotch, the same kind that all of us have passed through. You were born with it!"

Born with a crotch.

The men of my generation often kept the traditional attitude to women, with its double standard and fear of change. Poets were writing love poems, fortified by the thought of sweet, submissive wives and unselfishly devoted muses. Who would dream of writing a song of praise to a woman Member of Parliament, a female bus driver or a surgeon—to somebody who arrived home smelling of carbolic and corpses and who, in addition, might refuse to cook dinner.

There were, however, many exceptions to the rule among the younger men. I was lucky enough to meet some of them and feel a wealth of gratitude toward them. Not the ones, of course, who helped from above, pompously and patriarchally, but those who helped and encouraged alongside and also developed alongside. They gave and I gave, exchanging gifts as equals.

Maybe male fear of the mother, the devourer, is the cause of much agony of living together? Most men my age know that their unliberated mothers have suppressed, somewhere, their need of freedom, that right to take part in life and the world. With or without joy they have all sacrificed that right. Men justly fear this blocked need in women, sometimes unspoken and suppressed. Some base their fear on a bad conscience, others because they are the victims of their mothers' unwitting revenge. The imprisoned mother always metes out invisible revenge on her children. Or maybe it is "only" her fatigue that makes her repressive or "only" her nerves and worn-out soul. Her need to own and decide for the children, to bind and dictate to her sons, is often a substitute for an unappreciative husband. It is tempting to love and be loved by a male individual who is dependent on her love, especially when her husband lacks understanding and when the never-ending demands on her seem unbearable. It is a relief to have a daughter or a son to open up to, to cry with. A possession of her very own, somebody she has carried within her. The human being she always dreamed of loving is the same human being she unconsciously loves to death.

The time had come to push me out into the world. I was at an age to be confirmed. I was about to meet the heavy load of massive prejudice, moldy ideas and destructive commands considered suitable as introduction to anybody going out to meet wonderful and glorious Life. My meeting with the Reverend Mathzén proved to be unforgettable

Papa had decided to let me board—the motherless child—at a vicarage in Central Sweden.

The Reverend Mathzén, Jesper Johan, was about forty years old, with thick lips and a hungry expression in his ever-inquisitive eyes. He was descended from a long line of clergymen, a quite common phenomenon, as psychological patterns tend to remain just as a family likeness often repeats itself through generations. With the Rev, original sin had found a relatively innocent expression. He was remarkably sensual, with a taste for the erotic. He had mounted his wife so often that not only had she borne him twelve children but had given him all her youthful vigor and by now looked like a jug of blueish soured skim milk. As ill luck would have it, the Rev had grown up in a part of Sweden where Calvinism blossomed, if one can use the word blossom to describe anything to do with such a thoroughly puritanical and life-denying doctrine.

The landscape surrounding us stood in its full glory this summer. It is possible that all this beauty deepened the crack in his soul and made him increase the volume of his inner strict and harsh voice, as you increase the volume of a radio, in order to cool down the dangerous allure of lovely young girls and beautiful nature in combination. He had soon chosen his favorite pupils, the best-looking girls who showed some physical maturity, while the rest of us, unsuccessfully struggling through puberty, had to bear the brunt of his Doomsday sermons. On the few occasions he had something good and friendly to impart in his teaching, when he touched on God's charity and love—something he hardly ever did—then his greedy eyes would rest on the pretty girls; but when he talked of morality and behavior in the spirit of Jesus, he bored his hungry eyes into the less fortunate group, while the monotonous loud radio voice droned out God's commandments and rules as if he were reading the stock market report.

I got into his bad books from the start. I was inquisitive, impertinent and self-assertive. I questioned his statements, not to make him unpopular but to bring myself to his attention and make him realize that I was worth noticing. The effect was, of course, the opposite from what I had hoped for.

Jeanette arrived later than the rest of us, direct from a holiday in England. Like me, she lived in Gothenburg and our fathers had a nodding acquaintance. Jeanette received parcels from home each week with sweets and lacy underwear and other lovely presents. She easily outshone all of us in beauty and soon became the absolute favorite, but she was tough and the Rev could not subjugate her. She possessed a self-confidence that we lacked, and she had had a foretaste of her shining future with boyfriends, fast cars and smart parties. The Rev was heading for a case of unrequited love.

I was lodged in a very small, bare attic room. You had to cross a big spooky attic to reach the corner where a sheet of plasterboard constituted one wall of my "room," containing two beds and a chair. The chest of drawers stood outside in the dangerous darkness. Before Jeanette arrived, I had to stay in the attic on my own, but I pleaded to be allowed to share with her for the reasons that we were both speaking with a Gothenburgian accent, that I admired her and, most of all, because I was scared of the dark. To my great surprise, the Rev granted my wish. Somebody with a base nature might interpret his motives as protection against "the sins of the flesh," but a kinder view would be to see his decision against his puritanical and strict morality. He might have wanted to improve the immortal soul of the spoiled Jeanette by letting her share a room with a poor and ugly girl. Jeanette had no objections and we soon became fast friends, with my admiration for her paving a wide boulevard for our friendship. Jeanette introduced a zest for life, previously lacking in the vicarage. The brooding sensuality lay heavily on us, as in a hothouse or incubator, waiting for the day it would hatch in all its glory, bursting all obstacles. That day the Rev would spring forth with flowers in his hair, naked and magnificent, and dance across the rolling meadows in this beautiful corner of Sweden.

All this was an impossible dream. The illness had already taken root. The Reverend's internal and private voice of God had ordered that the desires of the flesh could only be satisfied secretly at night, as when the sewer rat sneaks out to couple with the grass snake in a deadly and furtive meeting.

Jeanette smoked and used makeup on the sly. She also talked a lot about boys and love. We read magazines and listened to the radio, all of it forbidden and sinful.

The Reverend's love for Jeanette made him blind to her faults and he blamed me for all the pranks we did together, assuming that I exerted a bad influence on his wealthy and well-born protegée. He had his revenge during lessons by giving me the most difficult questions. His scornful glance never left my hot and unhappy face with the round and wide-open eyes, eyes that knew too much about him and were precocious and penetrating. My eyes knew by instinct the difference between dark and light. He chewed on darkness as others chew on tobacco.

He loved to paint pictures of a sinner and show how our Lord treats a sinner: by throwing the Truth and the Word in his face to shame him, by lowering the Hot Sun of Grace like an instrument of torture and then, at last, by giving Forgiveness from Sin with a softly padded voice—a pail of ice-cold water poured over the unconscious prisoner.

Jeanette was not worried about the treatment meted out to me. She received admiration, devotion and friendship with all the natural grace of the lady of the manor, allowing her chauffeur to hand her out of the car. To defend somebody, to share the blame for childish games and pranks, to own up to anything was completely alien to Jeanette. The world was divided so that some people were rich and beautiful and therefore successful while others were poor and ugly and naturally could expect a rough ride.

The Rev was unsurpassed in his quest to detect all that was sinful and wrong. He somehow hypnotized us to do forbidden things. He was attracted to bad smells, to anything damaged concealed from view, the hungry thief who had stolen a crust of bread from his miserly household—while all the time his voice was booming with the strength of self-righteousness.

His many children tried to lie low like frightened rabbits against the walls, and we were rarely allowed to meet them. They stayed hidden in what seemed like a concentration camp. We had some contact with his oldest daughter, who received religious instruction along with us. She had inherited her father's thick lips and her mother's lifeless eyes. She was quiet and secretive but now and again she would suddenly burst out laughing or open her mouth for an unexpected stream of words, like an involuntary gush of vomit.

The youngest son enchanted me when he succeeded in escaping the family net where the other eleven were caught. He toddled happily on the lawn in front of the house—until he was captured again and punished for his *joie de vivre*.

The Reverend's eyes were glowing with ardor when they rested on Jeanette's dark curls. He kept paying visits to our attic on the slightest pretext. He came to turn out our light, like a watchful shepherd who looks after his sleeping sheep, to observe whether his sheep really are asleep or occupied with something excitingly naughty. We pretended to sleep and he stayed with melancholy and excitement in his wicked eyes. "Lord, take pity on sinners," they seemed to say. "Lead me not into temptation but let your punishment smite me if what I feel is of the flesh and not of the spirit." Jeanette had let the blanket slide down to expose her breasts through her sexy nightgown. It was cruel of her and had me utterly confused. Who on earth would want to show anything to that disgusting man with his sick eyes. My hair was still in pigtails and I wore nighties made of flannel, inherited from Mama. I was lost in romantic dreams, metaphysical and unreal, slowly making contact with a new world. When time is ripe, another life grows painfully out of a childish body: swellings, life moving back and forth under the skin as if the child has been taken over by some subterranean dragon or a fish jumping about, making hills where there used to be flatness.

The world was exciting and new and tempting. I could giggle hysterically for hours at something that sounded improper and rude, unable to stop until I often ended up crying instead.

Jeanette had outgrown this wearisome state and was cooler and in better control of herself, almost grown-up in relation to the other girls and the Rev. Her graceful body made one think of innocent allure and early flowering, her heavy eyelids and the knowing but childish smile seemed to be able to reduce our stern and punishing shepherd to jelly, the gluey kind you can pull and fold.

Jeanette and I decided to try to put a stop to his nocturnal visits. She was getting tired of the attention and I felt scared and persecuted. We decided to drive him away with gas. We stuffed ourselves with crisp bread the whole day, from the moment we got out of bed until bedtime. With our stomachs distended like bellows, we closed our bedroom window and then we let off. When we heard his heavy tread across the attic floor, we crept under the blankets to silence our laughter. We saw him take a backward step, hesitate and then rush to open the window. He turned out the light we had left on as extra bait and hurried away, his running ghostly steps swallowed by the dark.

That did put a stop to his advances. Jeanette was as good at farting as she was beautiful and she enjoyed our pranks as delaying action to inevitable maturity, the painful initiation to female suppression.

Frankly, there were more unpleasant than pleasant interludes during this time of religious instruction. I was used to debates on religion from home, where the discussions or quarrels served to channel many unspoken conflicts and problems. My views on the subject were already inflamed and I never lost an opportunity to contradict the Rev. Having been taciturn as a child, I now had the ambition to express my views to a larger audience, not least because the Rev openly treated me with injustice and disdain.

I kept asking him about sinful things and why they were sinful. Was it a sin to smoke? Why was reading magazines a sure way to hell? What was evil in listening to secular music? Who invented sin? What happens to a person who thinks and talks of sin all the time?

He retorted, abruptly and angrily. I kept opposing his ideas of sin, resolute and stubborn as an old goat. This was unspeakable behavior. Nobody had dared to question his opinions before. If he had declared anything to be sinful, that had to be accepted as gospel. I kept up my protests. He shouted: "This is sinful. Please God that the blind shall see one day."

The devil was behind those body functions that were sensual pleasures. "Gluttony—one of the seven deadly sins" he shouted while he looked crossly at me because of my large and expensive appetite.

The whole summer was swept in a cloud of fire and brimstone. I was the defender of light and joy. He threatened me with his talk of death and destruction, all that I had tried to leave behind. I fought for my life while the others were indifferent. What he talked about made no mark on them but fell and settled on me like old bird droppings.

The electricity meter sat in the attic room Jeanette and I shared and one day, when a thunderstorm was brewing, we inadvertantly turned the main switch off. Maybe we unconsciously wanted to commit a real Crime that we would have to Atone for. The atmosphere was filled with drama, with sin and punishment, with our shepherds wild but imprisoned passion that grew fatter although it screamed with hunger. We hardly dared to enjoy our food without feelings of guilt. Anyway, the food we were given was generally tasteless, to avoid spoiling us with sensuous and material pleasures.

That main switch became a turning point in my existence.

101

The whole day passed without the Rev finding the electrical fault and he ended by blaming the power cut on the Devil. When he finally twigged the simple explanation, the switch-off, his immediate conclusion was to blame it all on me. Jeanette never entered his suspicion. I accepted the full blame—you don't tell tales if you have grown up among brothers. The Rev telephoned my father, who arrived in low spirits. This made me feel very unhappy. The Rev implored my father to remove his depraved daughter. Thank goodness, Papa lost his temper at this point, and as he was thoroughly familiar with the word of God after years of Bible study, he could raise the question whether it was not the lost sheep that needed looking after. If anybody present really was qualified to judge between the guilty and the innocent. If the Reverend Mathzén considered himself on a par with God in the matter of sifting the wheat from the chaff, then Papa was willing to accept the judgment and remove his motherless child.

But it has been known to happen that the Devil succeeds in tempting the most unlikely, the fairest and loveliest of creatures, to commit acts of sin and the sweet little Jeanette was probably not blameless in this particular prank. If the Rev, being a servant of God, could persevere with a good conscience in his object to withhold the Grace, the Holy Sacraments, the Confirmation of one of God's children into the congregation of the Blessed, then the little Jeanette would have to suffer the same deprivations. Because he who is unjust will be judged on the Last Day.

When Papa had finished his sermon, the Rev was pale green and perspiring. Whether it was the fear of losing Jeanette or of God's Judgment or that Papa had gone mad, or possibly because he was impressed, whatever the reason, he relented with a "Hallelujah, God is great" and "Let us try once more."

What was left of that summer remains in darkness. The Rev treated me like air, foul air at that. To humiliate me, he told me which questions he was going to ask me at the final ceremony, in order to avoid a scandal, he said. As a matter of fact, I had more knowledge of the Scriptures than any of my fellow pupils, but only this summer, the last time before I took sin and guilt and

God and His rules and Scripture texts, bundled them all together and threw them into the black sea of oblivion. I wanted no more of sorcery and black arts.

This summer had made me lose all proportion, inner as well as outer. I was chubby like a seal, nothing boyish in the way I looked but definitely girlish. The photograph shows a pudgy girl with plaits and a frizzy fringe that looked like a juniper bush frantically hanging onto a cliff. I had the fringe to improve my looks and the plaits in reverence for Mama, who had wanted me to keep them and who might decide to walk the earth again, in which case I felt safer complying with her wishes.

My dress was too long, with pleats that made me look enormous. Jeanette, dressed in white lace, with black curly hair and large brown eyes, looked like a young bride and made the rest of us look like well-fattened calves beside a slender deer. The voluptuous face of the bridegroom, looking like a satyr, can be seen at the back. Only his cloth proclaimed his vocation.

The day of confirmation saw the Rev as a changed man. He looked forward to remuneration for his labors and God's rich sun was allowed to shine on all the sheep. No more whiffs of fire and brimstone, of sin and shame. Gone was the air of condemnation and spying and the harshly puritanical and mean look in his face. He waddled about, helping himself liberally to the homemade cakes and buns like some jovial baker. He made himself agreeable, talking to the exalted and the lowly, waving his glass of juice like a genial toastmaster. Yes, we were all a big happy family, hallelujah. He had taken his family out of wraps, given them a good dusting and was proud to exhibit them, blinking and snorting happily at the innocent remarks about his productivity.

Was not his wife's stomach bulging again? "Yes, well, it says in the Good Book that you should replenish the earth" he beamed, leering in Jeanette's direction. It certainly helps if you can think of something beautiful when you mount the Mount of Olives with the burning bush.

Papa was enjoying a cheerful conversation with his old friend,

Jeanette's father, when the Rev approached. Papa's face showed obvious displeasure, the sun stopped shining for a moment and the ground trembled under Jesper Johan Mathzén but he managed to shake off his uneasiness soon enough and with true hypocritical fervor thumped Papa on the back with a "How nice that your little scapegrace daughter has become a child of God."

I stared with incredulous horror at my Bible where the Rev had written words to remember. The blackguard had had the temerity to write in my beautiful white bible, a gift from Papa: "Burn the dross in your fire of chastity."

Part Two

I feel
my "I"
is much too small for me.
Stubbornly a body pushes out of me.

Vladimir Mayakovsky

Paris, end of January—a new year.

I think of "Victoria" tucked into six feet of snow. I can hear the wolves howling from the edge of the forest and I sense the deep solitude and serenity of the house. I want to be there, not here in Paris.

My soul aches every time I come here, to the city of anguish. It must be possible to coin innumerable poetical metaphors describing the "Capital of Pain." I have lived here, off and on, since the age of sixteen. I have felt my inner self disintegrate, and I carry scars from invisible incisions, experiences that are difficult to put into words. A state of mind, a harsh reality, as Céline might describe it.

Ugliness, brutality, heavy swollen bodies resting on the metro grills, a breath away from death. This city, aching in each cell, each nerve, living by the grace and damnation of God—still besieged by a Divine hierarchy.

Do I want to see the ugliness? Ugliness and beauty are indivisible and I do not wish to see the one more than the other.

I remember Parisian springtimes of my youth when poverty and brutality constituted the dark and frightening backdrop for the make-believe happy plot on my inner theatre.

Childhood left behind! Next stop—youth? No, I have left nothing behind but the years, the swiftly passing time and the too smooth skin. The pain remains, all the time, as when I was a child, when Mama died, when I was forced into my feminine role, at first gently then suddenly and brutally on all fours, naked—with a man heavy over me.

Going back in time is to create a pause before what comes next. To search for a place in history is to understand that you are part of the future, painfully struggling forth around you, together with and created by you. Yes, created by you if you dare to be responsible for your actions. I dare and sometimes I don't dare but in the end I dare. I feel this pain inside me before I know why it hurts and why I want to lose myself in the past. Now, at last, I can see it from a distance and begin to understand what has shaped me and what has damaged me.

It is not true that I lose myself in the past. The past is up to its old tricks, it loses itself in me: what is individual and highly personal in me, as a woman, has merged with the human condition.

A human being among billions, a grain of sand, a seed in a teeming jungle of vital forces and possibilities. The world contracts in agony and pain whenever an umbilical cord is severed. Liberation means cutting off and starting to grow.

I believe I am beginning to understand.

What has been happening during these last few months—when I have not had time, or rather, when I have not been able to allow myself the luxury to write what I want. Instead there has been the day-to-day writing for livelihood and immediate needs. Bread and butter chores, translations, articles. The ever present fear that I won't make a go of it. Tax debts. The notebook with myself divided into figures and sums, according to the wishes of the inspector of taxes, with everything I do written down. My life and my hours on a piece of paper that is, without a doubt, easier to handle than I am: insecure, blushing and angry in front of the tax inspector. But most of all *scared*.

I firmly believe that they don't even try to understand me. I want to pay, square my accounts. But I don't want to hand over my life and my creativity on their conditions. I can't be a book-keeper for the inland revenue and at the same time write books where I present ideas that are important to me. I would really like to communicate with the taxman, and I suggested once that one of them should come to Paris in order to check whether my declarations were correct: that you don't get a receipt at the post office or the bistro when you make a phone call, that you can't ask a French artist or, even less, a South American to sign his name on the back of the bill at the restaurant where you have invited him for an interview. When I try to explain, the inspector looks at me as if I had lost my reason and I often feel on the verge of doing just that when I enter the beehive of bureaucracy.

This can't be relevant, I hear somebody say. But it is, it all hangs together. Two months of living day by day among people who force me to hold back what is most important to me, my writing, my fight for insight.

During the last twenty years I have lodged all over Paris, mostly in hotels, small, dirty, poor; in rooms with space only for an enormous bed and a wall mirror. Only occasionally have I stayed with friends and then mostly those friends who once were poor and still could remember what poverty is like.

It seems a long time since I arrived as a fifteen-year-old to stay with a French family. My first visit lasted a month and I spent it in attacks of chronic disastrous diarrhea, in apprehension of the highly educated and nice-mannered people who tried very hard to understand me, this adolescent monster made up of fear, self-assertion, curiosity and death wishes. I wanted to die in Paris, crap myself to death, spew up my dead mother, my stepmother, my ugliness, the teeming streets, the Coca-Cola, the Louvre and the scorpions in the south of France, where my hosts had dragged me, far away from myself, my undefined longing and my grow-ing, devouring sense of reality.

It is odd that now, when I am about to describe this period of my life, I happen to stay in Paris—I am up against walls of terror. The only way of tackling the problem, I sometimes feel, is to pro-ject myself objectively against memory, trying to view the past with a distance created by fear. Could I make it easier by osten-sibly writing about somebody with another name, write about her in third person? But that would be cowardly.

As the book progresses, I feel I ought to ask the reader's forgive-ness for writing exclusively about myself, my dustbin, my sore toe, the ache in my left side, the split nails, the missing tooth . . . Although my ailments are mostly internal, not visible, at least not directly visible.

As a child I was instructed to be cheerful and a joy to others. Papa wanted me to write happy books if I had to write at all. The effect has constantly been the reverse. My writing gets ever more cheerless, but in reality I am working toward a "happier" book, by forcing my way through darkness like a snow-plow through dirty and heavy snow, fallen from an unlikely sky.

It was considered a duty not only to be cheerful but to be *Snäll*—a Swedish term of highest praise meaning Good. Girls, in particular, had to be good. Boys might need a "naughty" aggressive quality to be able to cope with life, to make decisions and lead, but even boys—well all Swedes—between bouts of aggression were expected to be good. To be "good" can mean a lot of things.

To be good is to pat somebody's cheek but it is to refrain from retaliating when somebody breaks your arm: it is to lie about the truth, to know your place; to lie back, close your eyes and think of Sweden when you don't want to; to obey. To be good is to get up every morning for thirty years and go to work without once questioning the value of the work, but not to demand your rights as long as the boss speaks with a silver tongue and throws office parties. To be good is to accept, without a word of protest, an inferior flat at an uncomfortable distance in exchange for your own nice homey flat. You are good if you give everything away, and keep asking forgiveness, incessantly, if you think you have been less good. To be good is to hide successfully that you are not good.

Good people tend to help tyrants to suppress, oppressors to ravish and murderers to kill just by being good and quiet. They think first and foremost of "the individual," and they cannot count further than "one." The demon drink has to carry the blame when goodness turns to wickedness. The good will probably get to Heaven when the wicked have spoiled the earth and the good always keep track of what is currently considered good.

I believe that my self-imposed demand to be "good" again played me a nasty trick; my stay in Paris, meant to promote work and worthwhile tasks, not least the writing of this book, was put to a severe test. I ought to have stated my opinions openly instead of keeping a cowardly silence about the crushingly repressive and chilly ambiance surrounding me. I should have written about it, at least, so that I could have progressed, however limpingly. But instead I let time pass . . . convinced that my unhappiness depended only on myself although that was not true.

I left Paris to go back to the house in the snow.

I left the town that always draws me back like an invisible irresistible current. I always know what to expect of pollution, excesses of all kinds, sleepless nights when all those arias come back to haunt me, the ones that I swore never to sing again but somehow sang anyway during the day's performance. Solo arias against a background of choruses and strange dramas where I am either dragged by the hair across the stage by a tyrant or covered with languishing kisses at the half-open window on the fifth floor.

I am increasingly tempted to take my place in the prompt corner, not only when Paris is the stage but generally, in my own opera performance, in my personal relations.

I want to sit in my corner and laugh at the prima donna, howling up there on the stage, the singer who is supposed to be me.

Because I am not at all who you think I am!

"A" believes that I am a bold extrovert, "B" is firmly convinced that I am his mother, "C" thinks that I am a schizophrenic and "D" that I am wonderful, which inhibits me with the fear of disillusioning him. "E" treats me like air and I whistle past him, trying to make myself heard, calling and shouting in vain. "F" is of the opinion and states openly that I am illiterate; I behave like an illiterate in his presence. "G" is something else again, he sees me as a body—with him there is no conversation, just heavy breathing. With him I rest my soul. "H" sees nothing but the soul, and in order not to frighten him I hide my body in tent-like dresses. "I" dissociates himself and I see him only through statements in the press. . .

It is wonderful to come home. Everything is white and still and after a couple of days I am white and still, too. My stomach has not recovered from all the cheap bad wine, but even that hangover is on the wane and I feel almost dangerously "normal" again, an indication that part of me is asleep. Imagine if the soul had arms and legs—in that case an arm or a leg is asleep. I can't bear to live with the whole me all at once, with the contradictory chaotic mosaic that is myself. It does not matter who you are but how you live. I have to shut the door on the chaos now and again and let myself emerge, little by little with extreme caution. I am like a six-year-old who tests how safe it is to enter the drawing room where the guests are by gingerly advancing with a leg or a hand—before the whole person dares to enter.

I am no longer the newborn innocent, growing straight, white and pure, waiting to be used. As an adult already sliding inexorably towards the dark ravine, the downward slippery slope, I am heavy with experience, memories, scars, hopeless happiness and lost faith. A compound of an old and a new person, a dress-up doll with a brand new outfit. A living creature with traces left by armies and sieges: burnt-out fires, violated ground with soiled snow, broken branches, rusty tins, excrement and blood. Springtimes have covered this ravaged landscape with mild, redeeming grass, with flowers nourished by hidden carrion or compost, with mighty trees in new leaf...This is myself at the age of forty. A deserted battleground where the grass has started to grow again... Only, the air retains a smell of gunpowder.

It feels restful to come home, to go into the nursery, to pick up the toys, to listen to the silent footsteps of the parents who disappeared into their mortal sleep long ago but whose steps I can hear as if it all happened yesterday. I hear her laughter and feel her long black plait on my cheek...and I am thrown high up in the air and back into Papa's arms, with dizzying and loving tenderness, maybe for a minute or two during my entire childhood.

I play with the fancy patent leather shoes that Auntie Tilly from Villa Björngården gave me, the hateful shoes causing so much envy all around me, the overlooked and spoiled little girl.

I hear screams coming from Hjorthagen, from the deer and moose in their confined artificial rut. The nights are filled with sounds: gales from the sea, riveting hammers singing against the ships' hulls in the harbor. I am there, here, everywhere, intensely conscious of the transience of all things. I must make good use of my life...my one and only Life!

Time of dissolution.

Mama was gone, the sound of her steps had died away, her pitiful sighs and moans were laid to rest in her coffin together with the long flowing hair and the folded cold hands.

Half a year passed. We tried outwardly to adapt to a new way of life, but disintegration, already crowned with success at home, continued its rampaging progress, slowly but surely. We still suffered, all of us, from the shock of seeing death in all its destructive reality. When it was all over, there persisted a feeling of unreality mixed with relief, but the shallow relief changed to anxiety at night.

Nobody knew what was going to happen, least of all Papa. He had lessons in ballroom dancing—being a practical and realistic peasant boy—and thought maybe already of acquiring a new companion. None of his children grudged him consolation, but when we realized the drift of his planning there was amusement mixed with some resentment. Not so soon, we kept thinking, let a little more time pass before she is supplanted. Mama had dramatically predicted in one of her outbursts that somebody else would take her place "before her body had grown cold." It was not that Papa had not loved her, and he certainly mourned her and missed her, but rather that he missed her acutely—she whom he had never really possessed. She had always been elusive, disappearing into her private world of visions and meditation. In isolated moments of passion she had left sin and guilt behind on her side of the bed and come to him, to make love without clasping her hands behind his back in prayer.

It was because he missed Mama desperately that he started looking for a new wife—and also for the sake of the two younger children, but mainly for himself. He had seldom dared to be alone with us children but had always approached us through Mama, and now he felt shy and awkward when he was suddenly confronted by a gang of demanding children who appealed to him in every possible and impossible situation. What was he supposed to say and do?

The oldest child was about to get her teacher's qualification and her first employment. The last years had made her stern, but she showed relief that the heavy burden of family responsibility was about to be lifted. She looked forward to the start of a normal life at the age of twenty-one, to be allowed to be young, to laugh and be a little light-hearted without the sobering thought that there would be "tears before the day was over," as her parents used to say. At last, permission to live.

The oldest son was doing his national service as a medical student and often brought home noisy and cheerful comrades-in-arms, talking of carbolic acid and corpses and "Rigmor Mortis." I kept wondering who this Rigmor could be. One day he brought home half a human skull, freshly sawed off, to be boiled and used as an ashtray. The sort of games that young medical students were wont to play with death to avoid being crushed by it.

The younger son often staggered home, dead drunk, after school dances. He had started drinking heavily during Mama's illness while he studied for his A-levels, which he passed with flying colors in spite of his drinking. He seemed to be living in a fog, and needed my help and support on his unsteady progress through the park, sometimes also to find the money for the cab to take his girlfriend home. We used to rest on a park bench and I collected the dew on my handkerchief to make cool bandages for his forehead to sober him up. I felt proud and happy to be needed. I, who was nobody, wanted to be of infinite joy and support.

One day she stood there, the unfamiliar woman my father had decided on. I tend to confuse days and months, even years for that matter, so when did the stranger arrive in our house? It seemed very soon after Mama's death, the year of mourning had not yet passed.

She was elegantly dressed, smart hats, furs and makeup, not

too much, discreet and ladylike. She looked like a real lady, the first lady I had ever met anyway. She was noticeably high-bosomed and dressed in gray, slate gray that looked well with her thick brown hair. She had large bushy eyebrows, inspiring respect and confidence—and her eyes underneath were inquiring, impenetrable and strong-willed. This was a woman very much aware of her place as a woman in the world, but not repressed—on the contrary, alive to the fact that the home was her domain, her realm with its concomitant rights and privileges. She gave the impression of being sensible, practical and tidy with a strong capacity for organization in the minutest detail. At the same time, she was willing to tolerate my untidiness—as long as I kept it to my own room.

The first meeting was awful for both of us. I had decided in advance to hate my stepmother and defend the mother I had never had. This new enemy was threatening to take my father away from me, and the combined misfortunes became too much to bear. I could only look forward to complete loneliness now that my sister was preparing to leave home, as well as my medical student brother; and my youngest brother had decided to sign on as ship's crew "to make things easier for Auntie Ruth." Only the baby was to remain at home together with Auntie Ruth's son, a soft-spoken and melancholy boy whom I liked at once.

I have never forgotten our first meeting, although the years that followed have given me a different and many times richer picture of my stepmother, who has good and bad qualities, like everybody. She experienced an immediate sense of insecurity when she became part of our family, and this forced her to restrain those qualities in herself that would have given me security: forceful sensuality and earthiness. On the occasions when she gave her sensuality free rein one felt that the wood floor might grow roots and start blossoming.

She was a masterly choice as an absolute contrast to Mama. Firmly earthbound where Mama had been confused and ethereal, practical where Mama had been wildly extravagant in cooking and dressmaking. Auntie Ruth did everything with confidence and coped with anything, from stuffing sausages to delivering babies. She saw at once what I lacked in the material sense, made sure that I was given a room of my own, a real girl's room with a kidney-shaped dressing table and lots of frills and furbelows. I was overwhelmed but still suspicious. She allowed me to dress fashionably and even to use makeup, where Mama would have gone to the stake to prevent me from tampering with God's "nature." I had weekly pocket money and could stop pilfering. She gave me a pair of beautiful green lizard shoes, and I soon learned to balance my still clumsy childish body on the high heels. The green shoes were hard-edged but wonderfully smart, maybe not perfect for me at the time but giving a distant promise that one day I would fit them. About a year later she gave me black underwear for Christmas and permission to stay out at night as long as I wanted. By this time I had begun to look for consolation outside home. I was fed up with listening to the happy couple's steps between their bedroom and the bathroom, I lying in my newly decorated, presumably sound-proof bedroom.

The happy couple with their rosy satisfied faces made me furious with jealousy and hate, and that did not promote a good relationship.

I did realize that I was less than fair, but I felt desperate and helpless and was totally unable to show affection to my stepmother—unless we were on our own, which happened very rarely. Then I could feel her sympathy and understanding but most of the time she was too busy with other things.

Sometimes she gave me clothes and presents, bear-hugs and big warm smiles—at other times she kept finding fault with my personal hygiene and with my improper habit of appearing at the breakfast table in my nightgown. Propriety was high on her list of virtues.

I believe that our first meeting, blighted by a ridiculous little episode, turned out to be decisive. That episode sat like a splinter in the foot making it sore and tender, and I kept prodding my sore foot because I wanted grounds for my dislike of this well-meaning woman, who had taken on our house of mourning with her salty and good-natured personality. I had the mistaken idea that it was a sacred duty toward my dead mother.

I am sure that my stepmother regretted her entry into Slottsskogen many times, but in spite of everything she managed to salvage something worthwhile. The woman I know today is more real as a human being, chastened in many respects but better informed, more alive and genuine than the dyed-in-the-wool Swedish, smart and merry widow I first met. That woman was used to expense account lunches, plenty of money and formal dinner speeches. She took a legitimate pride in her ability as a highly qualified private secretary with a sound and well-balanced business sense. Besides the son she brought into the family, she had two grown-up daughters who eventually became my friends. It was a well-known fact that her first husband had been a meek and gentle man, the absolute contrast to Papa. The union between Papa and Auntie Ruth developed into an interesting but painful marriage where both seemed to have chosen their new partners because they were completely unlike the predecessors. "At last I have found the right mate," they seemed to have reasoned. But reality turned out otherwise. Expectations were not fulfilled; the solace they had always looked for refused to present itself. Happiness tends to escape when you hunt it with a gun. Auntie Ruth and Papa realized soon enough that they were chasing a phantom, but they pretended otherwise for the sake of appearances.

Excitement was rife the first time Auntie Ruth was expected at home. The best table linen and Mama's silver cutlery from Germany, with the noble crest, were taken out, dusted and polished. Everything smelled of moth balls—it was ages since the finery had been in use; like us it was tainted with cancer. We had polished and cleaned, trying to remove the traces, but with scant success as it turned out. Auntie Ruth started the changes from the very first moment, rebuilding, reupholstering, throwing away or relegating to the attic. This was a sane and sensible reaction on her part, making way for new times and a healthier air. She had a balcony made—the one mama had always longed for—but she contributed a substantial amount of the costs from her own capital. We were aware of her generosity and we would never forget how she was willing to share her riches with us.

She came through the door in her smart suit and we were introduced one by one. I, in particular, was close to hysteria. Was she going to like me? This question has followed me throughout the years, like chronic bronchitis; would people like me . . .

Fine chocolates were served with the coffee. Auntie Ruth made her choice and placed it on her saucer. I followed her every move as if bewitched. How well behaved she was, how elegant and cheerful!

We left the coffee table and started, all of us, on a guided tour of the house. Plans were made, amid much laughter; new cupboards and curtains were proposed and described: "This is the perfect place for it, maybe . . . no, silly, not so close to the bed, near the window instead and it must be wine red."

After the tour, we returned to the drawing-room, the coffee and the chocolates. But what was this? The chocolate cream that Auntie Ruth had left on her plate had disappeared! "Who has taken it?" she asked sternly—and "Strange, I am absolutely positive I didn't eat it." My habitual feeling of guilt, the constant *mea culpa*, made me blush in despair. Maybe the dog...? No, he had been with us—but so had I. Very odd...she kept repeating while she looked at us children...I am absolutely *sure* that I left it here. The minutes stretched into weeks and months and years.

I never forgave her that chocolate cream, which she probably ate herself anyway. None of us would have either wanted to or dared to touch it, not "her" chocolate, not anything belonging to Mama's successor. That poor woman who was not even allowed to be herself—only a "successor." As time went on, her anger grew and she found many faults with her new family. Papa's children possessed every imaginable fault. We were "thoroughly bad, not like other children" was her constant refrain. She was right, we were all awkward in our different ways—but we had been allowed our individuality, for good or bad. The disintegration of our home life had probably given us some kind of freedom that was not included in our parents' original plans for child-rearing, for straightening of "crookedness." It was perfectly true, I thought, that other children, all-Swedish, were not quite like us but more endowed with "goodness." Good little Swedish children, sturdy frisky kids with twinkling blue eyes, eating their porridge with milk and jam. Good Swedes who "would not harm a fly." I ought to be like them, and I wanted desperately to be like them.

Papa had hardly ever talked about sex. Once in a blue moon he would adopt the stance of a preacher and dispense warning utterances on the general theme that "nice girls don't do it" and "it" was done only by affianced or preferably married couples. On this point he was slightly more liberal than Mama, who had insisted on chastity until the wedding night.

Papa had, at the same time, a healthy attitude to sex that seemed to contradict his strict puritanical outlook, and this combination of two mutually opposing character traits made it difficult to know exactly what to do and which directive to follow. Because you had to "follow directives." Adults always knew best.

Our home life was dominated by the rather wild conduct of my two brothers, and to this was added the lovesick behavior of the newlyweds, their amorous glances and Papa's eager appeals every night—to coax Auntie Ruth into bed.

I still "slept," not yet awakened, always dreaming and daydreaming. My dream man was a composite of different boys; he would love me for ever and he would *take me away*. The hero of my romantic dreams had to be able to take me away from home, that was his most important purpose in my life and my fondest wish. By now I felt the loss of both my parents, and I was living in a home that was disintegrating or, at the very least, acquiring a new and strange character. Dinner parties with loud laughter, smell of cigars and sound of music with Auntie Ruth as the star in the middle, surrounded by her satellites. I tried to conform to the jollity while a feeling of emptiness was growing inside me. Want of tenderness and love combined with fear of death woke me up every morning at dawn, after too few hours of sleep. I shook and trembled in my bed and when papa passed my door on his way to the bathroom, I often waylaid him to ask if he knew why. His explanation was always the same. Puberty, that's why. Everybody had to shake and was shaken by puberty. Later, when I was about fifteen, my particular private horror of death started to manifest itself and by then I knew what it was all about.

The fear has attacked me, awake or asleep, from that time and ever since: I feel myself burning, the heat so intense that my body involuntarily twists itself into an upright position while fear and pain invade my consciousness and I know with a black, dizzying mad insight that I am about to disappear, to be finished and extinguished without the possibility to cry or weep or defend myself. The attack is over as quickly as it began and I feel completely spent, almost dead. A symbolic exercise in death, year in and year out, unmanageable and unchangeable. It can start any time—when I am happy, when I am taking my siesta in the heat of the afternoon in Greece. Suddenly I feel torn to pieces, gasping for breath, hitting out and throwing myself at somebody who might console me; but before I reach that person it is all over.

I have always known that no consolation could alter the fact that I am a potential corpse, a human being on loan to life for a limited time . . . . Everything will outlive me, glasses, tables, chairs. I do not really exist because I am transient, soon to become dust and ashes.

Just as well to put an end to this miserable existence, I used to think during my depressive periods. There is no joy in living when you know how it will end. The end is inevitable. I dared not believe in God or life after death. Only when I started taking an interest in others could I see any meaning in life, even though fear of death and obliteration continued to follow me.

I needed love as well as comfort. My need was so deep and complete, it was like a bottomless well. Nobody was going to fill this craving for affection, this trivial longing for love, however far and wide I searched.

"You don't love me," was my standard reply when somebody had been trying to convince me of his love for the hundredth time. To get proof I had to test the lover, and as a consequence I invariably succeeded in chasing him off. I looked for confirmation that it was impossible to love somebody awful like me.

I see it all now, I understand my illness and I am able to think of other things, to stop whirling round on my subconscious merry-go-round. I can observe it from the outside, sometimes riding on one of the horses, round and round, but capable of stopping and getting down.

A line of communication has finally been established between the two sides of my personality, the conscious and the subconscious—a source of joy, to others and not least, and tragicomically, to myself of course. I can observe—but I cannot change as much as I want to. I can help others cross the street, help them with their visible and invisible burdens, but I still cannot help myself.

Papa and my stepmother used to go away for the summer during the first years of their marriage. That was the start of a long-desired freedom for the four of us. The house was large, surrounded by the lovely park where we could wallow to our hearts content in the rich sumptuous greenery. A small army of friends was brought into this haven, with their toothbrushes and other supplies. My younger brother had met other sailors when he was out at sea and they came, tough strong fellows, hard-drinking womanizers. My older brother brought home medical students and the chaps he had met doing his national service, and my sister took the opportunity to invite colleagues from the teacher's training college and other friends, now that she finally was allowed to mix in their company without awkward questions being asked. Now that she was an adult.

It was different for me. They allowed me to observe what was going on but on the explicit understanding that their assured privileges most certainly were not mine. At least not yet. All the same, I managed to have a lot of fun. I became their "mascot."

I remember one early summer's morning when a reed-thin girl, dragged home and used by one of my brothers, hurried away, exposed and crouching under the blinding light. She was pale under her messy makeup, dressed in black tulle, and her eyes were sad. A thin, black shadow flitting through the tall green trees. For the first time I felt deep compassion for a sister when I recognized the expression on her bewildered face and could see her disappointment that there was nothing more to this "night of love," that it had been reduced to one thing only. What she had left behind was typical male contempt for a girl who had given in too quickly—a girl who had been too easy.

Men did not like their girls to make a fuss, on the other hand. Petting was considered silly and dishonest. You might as well go the whole hog. Petting caused "pain" to the man, that was the accepted truth. Either you did "it" or did not start anything. Hypocrisy was nothing for them.

But when the girl had given in . . . . Well, it depended on her reputation, whether he had fallen in love, how the affair had started. Sometimes the signs were favorable and the girl was treated as a fiancée; at other times she was nothing but a worthless piece.

At some future time they were prepared to let me be kissed by a friend of theirs, but absolutely nothing more. Petting, frowned upon normally, was all right for their little sister.

I knew, however, where I belonged. My compassion for the abandoned girls was dimly perceived but unmistakable. I knew that I was about to join the ranks of the helpful girls, the ones who are willing to protect men from "pain," who don't make themselves out to be unduly important, who don't like hypocrisy. The girls who understand men and male needs because they dare to admit their own. That's where I belonged, among the fallen angels with whom I had always felt at home.

Frank was my deliverer. A fair-haired intellectual with finely chiselled features and spectacles, medical student and friend of the family. I was in love with Frank and also curious to know The Great Secret, about to be revealed. We had enjoyed some mild petting, more or less directly under my brother's gimlet eye, just so far but no further. I was confused, my state of mind swung between giggling and deep earnestness. My feelings were undecided; I could not take the whole thing quite seriously and it seemed farfetched, but I was able to kindle a kind of passion in Frank, a physical need that had to be satisfied.

I tried asking my best friend because I was a bit nervous about the *deliverance*, the giant step from heavy petting to the final world-shattering moment when walls tumble, church bells boom and stars fall from the sky. I had seen our famous screen lover, Georg Rydeberg, in the film *When Life Begins*, where he talks about the moon and asks the girl if she has noticed the sea lapping at their feet. When she replies in the affirmative, the lover, with tearful eyes, heaves himself slobbering on top of his beloved, who is very young and disappears almost completely beneath his padded shoulders. Sound effects, sighs, the sea fills the screen again, swelling and splashing and washing the rocks. The end result of all this water splashing is the girl's pregnancy. The lover fades away and it all ends very unhappily.

Frank had me worried. As our petting intensified, I was carried away by the unleashed passions and frightened by my own eager randiness. I gasped for air and felt quite sick with excitement.

I kept wondering if this was The Love that would transport me. Was this my chance to become the happiest and most beautiful of creatures? I had already planned our wedding, never mind that I was a minor and had to get special royal permission. My imagina-

127

tion enjoyed free rein and bolted into the universe dressed in bridal veil and all the trimmings. My imagination was boundless, as usual.

We started sleeping together in our separate sleeping bags when we tagged along with my sister and brothers and their friends and dogs to the family weekend cottage, always shivering from cold in the insufficient heat from a lethal smoking stove and always with the rain pelting down outside. The three guardians of my morals took turns keeping Frank and me under surveillance, to check that decencies were observed.

Finally, I could not help feeling sorry for Frank and decided to go with him to his lodgings one evening.

Frank had managed to remove the most painful obstacle on some earlier occasion; maybe he was not even aware of having done it but I had seen the evidence in my underpants. Penetration itself, the legendary entrance that he was the first to perform—felt surprisingly nice as well as painful. To receive a foreign body within my own, enclose it and keep it warm until I felt beside myself and wanted it to stay inside for ever . . . . That is how I felt, I was bursting with tenderness.

I whispered words that seemed to come naturally. I stroked his hair, I was his little sleeping animal curled up in his armpit. I played and I dreamed.

He said, "This can't have been the first time for you," and with these few words he let me crash down from the strange shimmering love planet, straight to earth, into a hole in the ground, a hole that took me months of climbing and scrambling to get out of. One could say that I was rather cut and bruised by my experience.

The considerably older Frank found a remedy for the attack of conscience that hit him—after he had reached his goal—by laying the blame on me, taunting me and putting me down.

My brother, brooding and black as thunder, was waiting for me one day when I came home from school. He looked brow-beaten and he obviously wanted to crack the whip over somebody else in his turn. He was brief and to the point: "Just like any whore."

The message was clear and crushed me utterly. I understood through my own shame and fear that it was rough on him. Frank must have spread some awful rumors about me. Everybody knew and everybody talked. My beloved brother was dragged in the dirt, his honor lost because of his sister—the common whore.

My brother eventually assured me on that score. Frank had told "only" him. But what about this thing I had lost, my precious virginity! I was measured against a scale of values and the balance was negative. I *had been* pure and now I was tarnished, fallen, smeared, soiled.

I realized that many emotions were involved. My brother loved me and that made him angry, ashamed, possibly jealous and, most of all, worried about me. He had always felt responsible; for years he had been substitute father and mother, showing his concern directly and seriously with many admonitions and sometimes awkward exhortations.

It was no help in this particular business that his best friend was the culprit who had failed his trust and, to add insult to injury, had embarrassed him by telling. I wonder *how* he told the story and what earthly purpose his telling had served.

Frank had the idea, maybe, that the two of them could share me, in some mystical way. I was no longer my two brothers' proud possession and little sister. The sharing-out process had begun, and in years to come I would have to split myself into more and more parts to be possessed by more and more people. In the end I was splintered in so many fragments that the whole idea of possessing was called in question—you cannot possess another human being but everybody is a mysterious nucleus of energy shedding particles of itself by radiating force. The right of possession need not come under discussion. I am allowed to exist as an independent physical unit, indivisible but generous with myself.

The affair with Frank precipitated a new crisis. One night I had reached the end of my tether and crept into my parents' bedroom. I woke Auntie Ruth and tried to tell her of my inner confusion. She responded at once, fully awake with her own soul bared, and everything that I had found artificial in her gone. Her spontaneity was intuitive, her hand caressed my cheek and she looked at me as if she really understood everything. Words were not necessary, she made me feel secure for a little while and she conveyed the knowledge to me that it was only a question of time until I myself would understand why I felt so scared. She made me realize that it was not one single cause, it was everything. All of life's misery—every night and every day.

I had no idea how to defend myself against all the tempting and cruel possibilities that surrounded me. Or to be more precise: I knew I would never be able to protect myself against my longing for human contact; I had no defense against destructive as well as benevolent forces. I have no protective skin, I have always lacked protective barriers as some people lack hair and stay bald. I was born without and remain without protection, as ever.

My brothers were not particularly tough or hardboiled toward women, on the contrary, they were rather soft. The most prominent characteristic of one of them was his wish to talk to the object of his desire. Not just chatting her up, but talking seriously, gave him the confidence to take her to bed. You knew what was cooking when you saw him, pale and tense, talking intently in a quiet corner.

The other was open and direct, easily excited. It didn't bother him why or hardly even with whom he fell in love, he simply turned on his considerable charm and warmth which made his victim fall into his arms with all the signs of lively enjoyment.

What I simply couldn't understand was their idle talk afterward. Had she not left the loving embrace but a moment ago? Could she have changed by leaving the room? Does the lover shrink after the embrace is over? Is the lover a danger again, after the act, is he or she a threat to get away from? Or is it the vain attempt to obliterate the picture of oneself reflected in the lover's mirror? I shall never understand myself or anybody else. How we tend to deride the person who just left the room, how this betrayal is a perpetual and unacceptable companion. Our excuse is that everybody does it without meaning any real harm. Maybe we are afraid of "ties"; we try to talk ourselves out of commitments and we prepare ourselves to cope with unexpected blows. We gird our loins against attacks and disappointments, against our too intensely burning love, an all devouring love. It is a vicious circle of sweet fearful betrayal creating new promises that in their turn beget new treacherous hopes.

I started alternating between toughness and bitter desperation. I dared not reveal weakness and anxiety. In school I showed terrible aggression towards schoolmates and teachers. I had one or two friends and one teacher who understood and helped me. In fact, she saved me.

Most nights I drifted around with a friend from Stockholm, a girl with exclusive habits who had a job and earned money but, like me, felt abandoned. She was sophisticated and experienced and she taught me how to use makeup, to dance and to dress. Under her tutelage I learned how to turn myself into a sex object. She arranged parties where I made myself roaring drunk on aquavit and juice and had to retire to the bathroom and stay in the tub until I had spewed up and sobered up enough to go home. This was indeed living life to the fullest, and it gave me something to brag about.

My memories are as dark as the parties I went to. Parties with lights turned off, music turned on, sighs from dark corners, creaking bedsprings, drunken laughter and groaning and underneath it all a bleeding desperation.

My life was a series of one-night stands without a trace of love. I was the archetypal chum and generous with myself but nobody was willing to answer my anxious questions. I was led to believe that it had to be like this if I wanted to be loved, or sometimes I made love because nobody cared a damn.

I was a child inside another person who was me as well. The child lay crouched in the fetal position, inviolable, waiting for the misery to end. Whatever happened—the violence and the betrayals, the love-making akin to rape—did not touch the child in me. That part of me could stand aside, watching and beating time to the drums and the shouts. I am sure that my experience was not unique but shared by many sisters and, maybe, brothers. The compulsion to act one way or another doesn't always come from the outside—more often from within. The tormentor inside is exhorting us to keep the very deepest unspeakable secret. Strong prejudice will not allow you or me to mention the silent violence we have been conditioned to accept or forced to endure because of pressure from outside and inside.

I know, however, that all erotic love need not be violent and submissive. Self-preservation had taught me to switch off, but I knew that I would be able to turn myself on again and open the door to a friend who might reach me with his love. I struggled to preserve my purity, the real important purity that was going to save the real important love, for me and for those I would love with body and soul undivided.

The prince took a very long time coming: he who was supposed to awaken the pathetic, hurt and inarticulate woman-child.

I used two different languages: one coarse, cheeky and aggressive for daily use, another for writing poetry. My two personalities were placed on either side of an enormous gulf—calling and insulting one another, one crying bitterly and the other full of contempt.

My notebooks allowed me to be the person who cried. She who wrote about what it was like "to live by halves." This gave me a chance to bridge the gap, to reconcile myself to myself, very slowly becoming *one* person with a dual personality but no longer two different people living different lives—like Dr. Jekyll and Mr. Hyde.

One who helped me to bridge the gap was Manne.

My sister had her first employment on one of the islands in the Bohuslän archipelago and I lost no opportunity to spend school holidays with her. Soon after arrival, she fell in love with one of the islanders and soon after that she married, against Papa's expressed wishes. Her husband, like my father—both were men of the people.

She soon produced twins and, after a too short respite following Mama's death was again tied to the kitchen sink with a double work-load as teacher and housewife. Money was scarce and her husband had difficulty finding employment. The island had a few quarries, a very small building industry and some fishing. Not enough to support a growing family. After the twins came two boys, one year apart. My sister labored, cried and gave birth. Later on she cried and labored and started shouting when her nerves gave out. Her husband, a quiet and kindly man, tried coping to the best of his ability but he was really up against it: their mutual differences, unemployment and, to add to that lot, society's hypocritical and condemning attitude.

I looked for a home and I wanted peace, that's why I went to stay with my sister, doing my best to help her with the children, changing nappies and taking them for rides in the pram. I can remember how I kept asking them to shut up but with very little success.

It was my considered opinion that nature had bungled by endowing kids with this talent for making dreadful noises. It was of no avail that I lifted them up because the minute they were back in bed, they started howling. I concluded that I must lack the maternal instinct so very evident in my sister, Irmel.

A summer with Irmel and her family, when I could shake off my home and my parents and the wild goings-on of my two brothers, was like a cleansing bath and the effect of it lasted several months. Maybe the sun burned the dross that the Reverend Mathzén had talked about, and sea water rinsed off the mud. The healthy and simple life, close to nature, reminded me of my childhood and felt like its continuation into adulthood. I had no need of entertainment as long as I could feel warm and secure in their family.

The quiet tenor of my life continued until a girlfriend took me to a dance in Hunnebostrand where I met Manne.

When you have tried to communicate with people for years without a common language, when you could have sworn that nobody saw or understood or even wanted to understand you—when you least expect it, you meet somebody you "have known all your life." A person who understands unspoken language and can see what is helpless or beautiful in you and even appreciate your compulsion to show your ugly side.

That person instinctively catches your rhythm just as you catch his or hers, neither of you knows or cares who sets the tone, nobody is subordinated. You are equal and speak the same language. He looks exactly as you always knew he would look and you are perfectly confident that you are as he wants you. Neither of you have to make an effort, you pass without a test, you are banded together without a conspiracy, you grew up together without knowing it, you won't ever have to explain yourself. If there are differences, both of you rejoice in the similarities too much to notice them, at least not for a long time.

This belonging together is called many things. Some call it love until the day they go their separate ways, then their legs carry them off in different directions and they who belonged together cry without knowing why. But it is the price they have to pay to go on living. Only the stubborn refuse to recognize what has become petrified and invalid, nothing can stop or alter the process of leaving one thing for another. When new love enters in full cry, the next parting is there, waiting.

Manne was leaning against the wall of the dancing pavilion. He was good-looking, not really my type. The lookers usually frightened me.

I had been mildly in love with a fisherman who was also a bird-watcher, of feathered friends. He could whistle and mimic bird calls like nobody else. He spoke with a strong regional accent, was fond of aquavit, kind and amusing. He never expected me to sleep with him. Before the bird-watcher I nurtured a distant love for a taxi driver who was athletic with a classical profile, took snuff and knew everything worth knowing about Life. Of all the islanders I got to know, the mystical and attractive sailor Black-Alfred was the most dangerously exciting, with his worn and haggard face. He played the concertina and sang "Maria Maruschka from Petrograd . . . " with a boozer's gravelly voice. He was much older than I and therefore nothing could, or did, happen between us, but that did not stop my attraction, my strong pull toward him, he who had experienced a lot and who was the most tenderhearted and considerate of men, surprisingly enough.

Black-Alfred, another friend and I went fishing for sardines early one morning in Gullmarsfjorden. The sheer beauty of the scene completely went to my head and I felt like jumping overboard. Black rocks descending abruptly into the sea, the sun on the horizon, the hint of warmth and the fish glittering in the net.

The wind rose on the way home and I treated my friends to a free show. I staged a funeral at sea in my own typical style with a taste for the macabre. I wrapped Black-Alfred in the Swedish flag, put a hymnbook between his hands, sang "Morning in the Mountains" with the tears coursing down my cheeks while the corpse underneath the flag laughed fit to bust. I declaimed with pathos on the subject of a sailor without a harbor, who will safely reach port and find eternal peace on the heavenly shores.

Black-Alfred at sea, in stormy weather, at his own funeral on a small boat. Black-Alfred soft as clay in the hands of a fifteen-year-old rag doll in the midst of idyllic Bohuslän.

Manne wore spectacles, was fair, tall and very serious. He had a sensitive mouth and large green eyes underneath perfectly straight, black brows. He looked straight at me who was hideously ugly and neglected and I almost collapsed from fright at the thumping noise in my breast.

He asked me to dance and I stumbled along. Then, suddenly, everything fell into place and the noise inside the ribcage ceased. I could hear our voices quietly discussing personal matters that normally made me flustered and shy. We talked about poetry. It turned out that he wrote, too. Nobody, except my sister and brothers, and now Manne, knew about my writing. We talked about books, another topic seldom broached in public. We discussed our parents in all their general awfulness, our plans for the future and what we wanted from life. We felt secure enough in each other's company to reveal our inner selves—usually kept hidden from fear of being ridiculed.

Instead of going home, I phoned Irmel and asked her permission to sleep overnight in Manne's home.

In all respectability, I slept in the basement and Manne had his bed in the kitchen above. His parents, who were tourists from a town in central Sweden, slept still higher up.

Manne's father taught physical education, had a big red nose and seemed to me kind and broad-minded, an opinion not shared by Manne, who found him hard and demanding.

I daresay that Manne was right, but when his father looked at me, his eyes grew moist and very warm. His mother was kind, talkative and submissive. Mother and son were united against the father.

They wanted to keep me with them; the basement room was at my disposal. Was I allowed? Did I want to?

I shot home to Irmel to pack my things and returned to my new home with her blessings. Permission was not necessary, nobody to ask permission of, really. I had to be trusted to know what I was doing, as nobody else had time to spare looking after me. After all, I was fifteen and soon, in August, to be sixteen and I could stand on my own two feet. "A little lady" said the older ladies. "Precocious" said my three siblings.

Manne wanted to make quite sure that I was not to disappear, so he came with me to Irmel. He was as much in love as I. This was Love with a capital L, I believed at the time—as always. And it was. Love at fifteen. Love for the first time.

Manne soon moved into my basement room. We kept our door open to the meadow and the green tall grass invaded our living space, covering the walls, spreading wild flowers across the blanket and in my hair. The scent of yellow bedstraw pervaded the air. We lived in the meadow and made love with it.

Our love was romantic but sensual as well. I had remained un-awakened in spite of my experiences but now I encountered sensuality as a gentle caress on my skin, like a sudden hot puff of wind stirring the sand.

My dark anxiety, my guilt feelings and self-torment disappeared. I no longer need feel debased, love had purified me. I had complete confidence in Manne and that made me open and positive to the world at large.

Summer winged its way through the leaves and the grass. Soon it would be time for me to go to France in order to improve my French, but I didn't want to leave. I wanted more than anything to stay, growing like a fetus in summer's green womb with the right to be born again to brighter views—to better conditions.

Manne was heading for the university, in Uppsala, while I had to look forward to two long years at school when I indeed felt ready for marriage and a life with Manne until death would part us.

We had already acquired habits, trying to assert our separate personalities with cautious quarrels. Manne tended toward a certain stubbornness and pride as I tried to secure benefits for myself with the help of overwhelming benevolence. Because I was starved for love and tenderness, I grabbed for it and at the same time started to build fences around us. We were both narcissistic, lived spontaneously and generously in our private world but looked at ourselves from the outside and loved what we saw: two lovers.

Separation loomed, We stepped up our quarrelling—from fear

and anxiety. Nobody knew what was going to happen. Our life needed structure, it needed to be shaped like a lump of clay. We made and retracted promises. Manne worried and wrote solemn prose poems to me, on our future together: "If we can't get on now / how will it be in future? / When we can't seek shelter in summer / when the roots of the jungle can no longer soften our steps" . . .

There were fundamental differences between us, male versus female. Men apparently find it easy to relinquish feelings and view a situation objectively, through a looking glass or a microscope. It seems as easy for them as jumping out of bed into the shower each morning, soberly and with a minimum of fuss. I was different, trapped by my feelings.

He kept testing the strings that tied us together to find out how far he could stray before they broke, and if they broke . . . how much was it going to hurt?

He never strayed far and he always returned, observing my reactions with some trepidation. I was the supposedly unstable partner who might try to end it all by drowning just to shorten the agony of waiting for the unavoidable end. I knew a lot about the finality of death.

I wanted to get deeper into our relationship with the same impatience that often forced me to hasten destructive processes. Not this time, though. This time I wanted to savor our unity to the full, to learn to know Manne before it broke up and the miracle dissolved and vanished. I wanted it to be realistic like autumn and winter—not this green blissful summer's fairy tale that nobody could take seriously.

The day before my departure we went out in the skiff to one of the rocky islets and dropped anchor close to the shore. We started early in the morning, planning to stay away all day. Now when I write about that day, all the details stand out in my memory with a frightening clarity.

At first we just rambled, doing nothing in particular, swimming and sunbathing. Our islet was one of hundreds similar to it in Bohuslän. We felt we needed to get away from his over-protective parents and be on our own. That day we belonged together in absolute harmony. Manne entered my soul with positive loving force, pushing out the part of it that I thought of as sickly. His love was completely unreserved and penetrated so deeply that I have ever since longed for the same feeling of almost criminal simplicity and innocent trust in another human being.

We swam and made love and when we had exhausted ourselves and explored all possibilities and still didn't want to go home—my breast was heavy with unshed tears and joy at the same time. I wanted to see what flowed out of Manne—as if that would reveal the alchemy of his soul and solve all the riddles.

So—with the strong sunlight smarting my eyes—I started caressing Manne—and his response was immediate and visible. I caressed him until he practically shouted with sensual pleasure and he let me have free rein. He understood my feelings and my need, everything about me, and he gave himself up to my ministrations with a tenderness keeping pace with his heightening passion. When he finally stretched out and let his seed erupt with violent magnificence, I felt cleansed—I understood then and forever that sensuality is as pure and natural as when a cat licks his fur in the sun, as necessary as rain and fire: unassailable and simple, independent and free.

The day came when I had to leave for Paris and the south of France. We parted with holy promises of eternal faithfulness. Our love had never been stronger than at that moment, as if we knew we were saying good-bye for ever. My stay in France was marred by my intense feeling of loss, by a black melancholy only occasionally relieved by illness. Then I would let nausea and dizziness take over and wrapped sickness around me like a cloak. I felt sick and scared, a surfeit of pommes frites in Paris and scorpions in the beautiful province of Vaucluse.

Papa wanted me to improve my French and arranged, through a friend of his with business contacts in Paris, for me to be a "paying guest" in a French family, a guest who was willing to lend a hand with the domestic chores.

I found myself in a highly intellectual family of committed socialists who seemed to be able to combine ideology with business, investing and managing foreign capital. Their daughter was one year older than I, an incredibly beautiful girl, as intelligent and ambitious as she was good-looking. She gave me a solid inferiority complex with all her accomplishments. She studied at the university, looked after a child fostered by her wealthy parents and was able to discuss philosophy with an old professor from the Sorbonne—as if she had been born with extensive knowledge of Socrates and Plato. She and the rest of the family looked at me with a mixture of horrified wonder and compassion. The clothes I wore, presumed at home to be the latest French fashion, just looked tasteless and vulgar in Paris.

I had fondly imagined that I looked smart, but the minute I arrived at Gare du Nord, the scales fell from my eyes . . . not to mention how I felt when I stepped into the bastion of refined breeding and exquisite taste. They believed in understated elegance; makeup was taboo. I had never been taught these aristocratic modes of behavior and appearance and I have never been willing to accept them. These people gave the impression that highborn means born beautiful. Madame was a Russian aristocrat and her first husband, also of noble descent, had been a French consul somewhere in the Orient until his death. The daughter was her first husband's. Her present husband, "Monsieur," who was considerably older, occasionally teased Madame about her big stomach, the only vulgar contribution to the dinner conversation. When teasing, he always added the information that many famous artists tended to depict their models with big stomachs. Madame used to blush when she tried to hide her anger; sometimes she cried. Other topics of conversation were socialism and communism, Sartre and literature. I soaked it all up like a sponge together with the invaluable instruction to visit bookshops. As I was already bilingual, I quickly learned to speak French. Acquiring knowledge has never been too much of a problem for me as long as I am not force-fed under degrading circumstances.

Very soon I felt great affection for Madame, who was well-meaning and kind. Monsieur could have been carved out of stone with his Freudian beard and his frightening authority, heavy and impenetrable as a medieval castle wall. It was impossible to breach that wall and live. Irène, the daughter, was the family jewel. She was mild and good, musical and intellectual, pure and intelligent—she possessed all these attributes through and through and through. She had never, seemingly, been in doubt about her role in life, about how to act in order to achieve maximum success. In comparison with her I had no defenses, no French, no education, no beauty. But I was amusing and it was not long before I had them laughing at my antics, in spite of my feeling unhappy and homesick. I mimed and mimicked, performing symbolic somersaults in French. I was wonderfully helpful, I who normally at home locked myself in the loo to get out of doing household chores. They wouldn't let me pay for room and board, refused pointblank to take any money, though the amount of work I did in return was laughably minimal. They had servants, but Madame did a lot of the cooking herself. There was wealth without ostentation. They held work in high regard and were not in the least snobbish. Their principles on equality were of the highest order even if the very best socialist intentions hardly removed all upper-class traits. Class-consciousness hung like delicate and discreet lace curtains in front of the opened windows, and in the background was the wine-red velvet that had collected dust from the decadence of earlier generations. The ambience of the upper classes was everywhere: in their wealth, in their intellectual refinement, in the way they looked at class, in their high moral principles—only people born and bred with privileges take them for granted.

The flat, on three levels, was situated in St-Germain-des-Prés. The loo was on the second level, my room on the third, and I scuttled like a yoyo between the floors on account of my nervous stomach that protested violently against the unfamiliar food and my insecurity caused by the strange atmosphere. I had diarrhea and felt sick all the time, day and night, with Madame wondering why and Monsieur observing me closely and asking with some suspicion whether I was on drugs. Irène pretended that the problem didn't exist and talked about philosophy. I kept dropping curtsies, played the fool and sat on the loo.

We were to spend a few weeks with an elderly sculptress at her country house in the south of France. The sun was burning hot, the air stood still, and in the evenings Irène used to sit under the trellis with its luxuriant exotic flowers and sing Russian folk-songs with a wonderfully clear and pure voice. The sculptress was kind and eccentric. She and I exchanged smiles instead of talking. There was a small green, rather slimy, pool where Irène crawled around in the company of thousands of tadpoles every morning. I kept to the shade as much as possible, staying in my bed on the top floor and feeling sick, while something rustled alarmingly in the fireplace. A big black scorpion lived in the bathroom.

I alternated between writing despairing poems in solitude or sitting shitting on the loo. It has occurred to me since that I might have profited more from my stay if I had made more of an effort, but I guess I managed to learn quite a lot all the same.

I learned to like the family but I didn't admire them, thank God. I was aware of their flaws from the very beginning. I could see the innocent hypocrisy in Irène and the way Monsieur loved money and property. I felt a warm and deep gratitude toward Madame but I noticed how she was trapped by her aristocratic pride, however much she talked about equality and human dignity for all. One day she started asking me about mama's family name—de Grahl—and she really wanted to know everything about the family, for no other reason it seemed, than to elevate me into a higher category that would excuse my presence in the eyes of their aristocratic friends. According to her, I was not as ugly as I imagined—I just didn't know how to dress and how to make up. I was primitive and chaotic as a person, with my sudden attacks of shyness that made me clumsy and awkwardly nervous.

Madame had a brother who was roped in to show me Paris, or more precisely, the Louvre, where I was force-fed culture day after day. Night after night, after the late dinners, El Greco and Goya appeared in nightmare visions between my violent convulsions of nausea. I was a diligent pupil, however; I wrote down the names of the artists and learned much that would stand me in good stead when I returned to school. But I didn't *see* the works of art until years later when I found the way on my own to the Louvre. Of all the museums in Paris, my favorite has always been Musée de l'homme where the human being is the main theme and where human life and culture, past and present, is displayed and expressed in an immediate and direct way, like a handclasp or a box on the ears.

Madame's brother hated his onerous task but obliged from a sense of duty. He teased me all the time, flirtatious and furious by turns, and grew increasingly irritated with my heavy, bad-tempered and disapproving attitude. My feet hurt but he would not let me rest, the blisters reduced me to tears but he only teased me about being "lazy." I clenched my teeth and vowed to have my revenge. The object of the exercise was to stuff me with culture through suffering, to the extent that he even grudged me a refreshing drink after I had been sweating for hours and hours on my tired feet.

In the metro on the way home, he said that I was "terrible" in a loud voice, which caused me to blush with shame and made our fellow travellers snigger with glee. A moment later, when the train passed a row of enormous posters advertising cheese, with the picture of a gigantic laughing cow, *La vache qui rit*—with a big snout and an enormous mouth reaching from ear to ear—I pointed at the cow and said loudly, without mercy, in my rudimentary but effective French "*C'est toi*" "that's you," and the fact is, he did resemble that cow. The likeness was so striking that the crowd in the metro immediately perceived it and burst out laughing. My guide turned purple in the face and from then on I was spared those cultural and painful excursions.

At that age one changes rapidly and imperceptibly. When I returned home after six weeks, I was not the same person as when I left. I was on the whole slightly more discreet—outwardly and inside. I had learned skills that made it easier for me to cope with the outer reality. Madame cried when I left, I felt that she genuinely liked me as I liked her. Their love for the intellectual and spiritual life was something I recognized from my mother, and that had created a feeling of belonging and security and curiosity in me. Maybe these territories, as yet unexploited, were waiting for me to explore them, since they belonged to one and all.

My suitcase was full of books and my head was full of French words and sentences. I had seen how other people live and how, as a stranger, one can approach them and be accepted by them.

If only Manne could have been with me to share this experience. Instead, when I was back home, we had to content ourselves with phone calls and letters. Later in the autumn I hitchhiked to Uppsala with a girl friend.

We had both changed. Manne was studying law, he seemed new and strange and so did I. After that brief visit, we didn't meet until he invited me to the celebrated spring ball in Uppsala.

I was terribly nervous and would have liked to skip the ball and be alone with Manne as we used to be, that summer long ago. But instead we were surrounded by students and dancing and revels and friends and varsity jokes that went over my head. There were competitions between the student houses, stories about academic eccentrics and, worst of all, a deadly "in" jargon that left me out, inarticulate country wench that I was, much too mature and at the same time, too childish.

Very late, when the party was over, I crept into the kitchen and sat in the dark, shaking so much that I thought in the end that I was dying. Then I knelt, praying to God who was stone deaf and didn't see the crouching creature on the ice-cold floor. I prayed to the blind God, who slept. I prayed for assurance that love was not over, that life was not over, that warmth would return, that words would find their proper meaning, that the bed would not be so unwelcoming and Manne not so absent.

The years of instruction.

I had the reputation of blockhead at school, at least where arithmetic was concerned. I was nervous and insecure or possibly suffering from mental blockage during math lessons. My older brother was kind enough to collect a basketful of apples from the cellar, which he scattered on a table. He then asked me to add or subtract, ad infinitum. In his effort to make instruction crystal clear to me, he kept moving the apples about, arranging and rearranging them in groups of two or three.

I sat staring at the apples like somebody bewitched and couldn't, for the life of me, understand what he was talking about while he handled these perfectly ordinary pieces of fruit. What was he driving at with his "if I give one apple to uncle Sven, how many are left?" I couldn't figure out what was expected of me and what I could expect, a kick in the pants or idle teasing. After a while he shook his head and pronounced quite simply that "you're such a bonehead, there's no point in even trying." I believed him and stopped trying.

As time went on, I completely lost interest in the subject, which was a great pity because mastery of mathematics meant free entrance to the world of the "intelligent." Without maths, one's prospects were limited to a career in the practical field, especially if one was a female. Females ought to be hopeless at maths and reasonably good at languages, a safe and satisfactory state of affairs.

Every year I failed my exams and had to sit them in the autumn in order to be moved to the next form. Every year I preferred to take it easy during term or I simply didn't have the strength to stay alert during lessons because I had to be on my guard against mob rule and aggression. Every summer, a few weeks before school was due to start, a teacher or some other friendly person had to be found, somebody able and willing to help the poor half-witted child. More often than not, my extra teachers were more able and less stressed than the ones school provided and with their help I could make up for lost ground and achieve a pass.

During my first five years at the girl's secondary school, I stayed below rather than above average as a pupil. In the sixth form I was lucky enough to get a teacher who not only understood me but appreciated me, my essays and my arguments. She taught Swedish literature, philosophy, psychology and religious education, that is, she was required to teach us the minimum included in the syllabus.

She won my trust and I felt confident enough to show her who I really was and what I, in secret, was reading and writing. I actually found myself listening to what was said at lessons, which eventually had an effect on my grades. When I left secondary school, my final grades were good enough to secure a place at gymnasium.

My progress through the jungle of learning had been uneven and laborious. I thirsted for knowledge but I was confused and often on the wrong track, with a tendency to pass by brimming fountains that might have slaked my thirst in favor of rather muddy trickles of water.

I had access to the classics at home and read with eager interest Dostoyevsky's *The Idiot* and Tolstoy's *Anna Karenina*. Anna Karenina, in particular, became the glorious pattern for my dramatic portraits of tragic women. I was wont to improvise with tearful and pathetic recitations to an audience of family and friends, wrapped in fur-lined garments I had found in mama's wardrobe, while I sweltered in the summer heat. On one occasion it nearly ended as disastrously for me as for Anna Karenina herself.

We were at the seaside. Among the guests were Auntie Ruth's daughters with their husbands. Everybody had been drinking a lot, myself included—too young, too soon, as always. It was time for the show to begin. I fetched my Karenina costume, balanced a fur hat on my head—disregarding the heat of the day—and entered my inner theatre. With a voice muffled by tears, I declaimed about my lover abandoning me, about faithlessness and deceit. As the performance rolled on, I left the inner for the outer theatre where, for once, the audience was enchanted and attentive, firing my enthusiasm with their applause. After my solo performance, when I had rushed down to the shore in floods of tears and was poised to throw myself into the water, a son-in-law of Auntie Ruth's caught me at the last moment. He was the only spectator who had understood that something was very wrong. The others thought it was all part of the act.

The literary diet of my early teens was a muddy stream of countless romantic short stories in the weeklies whose content I mercifully soon forgot while they left a residue of sickly and unrealistic hopefulness. The man with steel-gray eyes and rippling muscles was my constant bed-fellow for years. When I was sixteen, the attraction of pulp fiction had already palled and I was pulled anew toward the shelves that housed serious literature. I burrowed through the books like a mouse. I devoured German heroic legends, continued with Thomas Mann, sank my teeth into the life of Buddha, into medical text books—with concomitant attacks of hypochondria—made forays into the Arabian Nights, had relapses into Girls Own type of stories and then to Hedenius' *Faith and Knowledge* if for no other reason than to plague Papa with sharp and shocking statements and turns of phrase from a book he had been given as a Christmas present but hadn't found time to read.

On one shelf stood Goethe and Schiller, von Kleist, Heine and Nietzsche, Rilke and Hölderlin. It is difficult to imagine more outstanding poets than these but for me, who had been forced to listen to my uncles reciting the famous lines ad nauseam, in dinner speeches and other German, yes dangerously German contexts, they were—taboo. German writers could conceivably turn out to be German murderers. To me they were representatives of an idealistic and dishonestly inflated male literature, flapping above my reality on steel wings of heroic rhymes. It took a long time before I learned to love Heine, Rilke and Hölderlin, but they have come to mean much to me. I can thank some of my teachers and friends for the gifts they bestowed on me, years later, by leaving the books, casually, on my table. That way they bypassed my pathologically defiant and suspicious attitude toward anything forced on me and opened my mind to new and fruitful experiences.

My two brothers counted artists, journalists and other intellectuals among their acquaintance, and I found faithful and encouraging allies in this group. One gave me the books of Ekelöf and Lindegren together with a collection of essays on the so-called "Writers of the Forties"; another gave me the novels of Olle Hedberg and a third carried me off on an all-consuming passion for Strindberg. For a number of months, I tried to emulate Strindberg, scourging my contemporaries with his help, venting my spleen upon scheming, foolish but dangerous women. He and I shared the blissful sensation of being Alone and misunderstood and wronged and persecuted—but a genius! The first essay I wrote that was given any general and favorable attention had Strindberg as its subject.

My opinion of Strindberg has changed since then and is ambivalent. His view of women makes me angry and despairing but I love his "fire," his courage and his clear vision.

Slowly I began to come to grips with the worst and the most obvious feelings of insecurity and slowly I began to gain confidence. I started to believe in what I thought was "myself." Papa didn't share my belief. He had an unshakeable opinion of women's rights and duties, what they ought to learn and to like. About "the youngest" he was absolutely confident that he knew what was best. I ought to get married, that was supposed to give me a sense of security. If worse came to the worst and nobody "wanted me," he envisaged a career as a primary school teacher, provided I was smart enough, or kindergarten teacher. It wouldn't be such a bad idea to learn how to cook or weave or look after children. It was important that I have a trade or a skill to "fall back on." My fondest wish was to become an actress but I kept putting off the unavoidable confrontation with Papa.

Both my brothers belonged to the students' Film Club and my older brother was willing to bring me as his guest. I took one mighty leap from Jeanette McDonald and Nelson Eddy singing and languishing about "sweet mystery of life" in It *Happened One Spring* . . . over to Bunuel's *The Andalusian Dog*. I still haven't recovered from the shock and Bunuel is and will always remain my favorite artist. He awakened me socially, politically, poetically and psychologically more thoroughly than any work of literature or person has ever been able to do.

I saw many good and highly accomplished films, classical works by Pudovkin, Eisenstein, Pabst and Fritz Lang, experimental films that turned my world upside down and made me forget who I was, not even care who I was. I immersed myself in the films and that in turn further stimulated my interest in books, gave me courage to take part in discussions and express points of view. I learned to criticize and "analyze" films, ridiculously faltering and unsure of myself, influenced by others—but on my way, finally launched on new adventures.

The year between sixteen and seventeen saw me develop faster than ever before—yes, faster than I had developed during all the preceding years, it seemed.

It was not only the Film Club but also new friends and new ideas that helped to break into my egocentric world. One of my teachers had given me a much needed push, but even more important was my friendship with a girl, one year ahead of me at school, who was assistant librarian and member of the school dramatic society. She became my support from the very first time we met at the library; we shared an interest in theater and film and she introduced me to friends of my own age.

Her name is Tua and she stood by my side when I, in fear and trembling, had to change scene from the unreal circus where I had played the fool to Reality, where I was expected to take life and the world and myself seriously, where others beside myself were of equal importance, where I learned what was happening outside the narrow confines of Swedish society.

I learned to temper the aggression that had kept my school-mates at a distance and made friends among them instead. I grew and developed by leaps and bounds, saw new possibilities stretching ahead and wanted to be involved in them all.

The time was approaching when I would have to decide what to do after school; by now it was a question of weeks. I had been tip-toeing around the problem—like a cat circling a bowl of very hot porridge, the porridge being Papa. I wanted to have my wish granted, to "study drama" as I called it. You didn't *become an actress*," you studied drama—that sounded more appropriate.

Tua was heading for drama school in Stockholm and I wanted to go with her. It was an ever more appealing thought, to be allowed to leave home and all the recurring problems, the increasingly painful arguments and psychological pressures.

Papa was getting tired and depressed by the bickering going on between me and my stepmother. Keeping pace with my new interests was loss of the affection she had felt for me earlier. She seemed to be of the opinion that I only pretended to have such interests, that I tried to make myself *grand*—a favorite reproach of hers. I am sure that I was quite unbearable as a new convert to intellectualism but I had to listen to constant jeremiads like—no point in getting on a high horse, plain common sense is the best qualification, good manners maketh man or as in this case, woman.

The honeymoon was over for her part, she sounded disappointed and sad when she talked about Papa. Sometimes she talked of "drowning herself in the little forest pond," at other times she could cry for hours and days on end. Papa said that it was "the menopause," as he used to say "puberty" to me and "only nerves" when Mama was unwell. He was no exception from the rule. In the male world these evasive phrases abound, to protect men from having to cope with a cumbersome emotional life and troublesome unmanly personal relations. Men much prefer abstract and objective ways of reasoning.

It was obvious that Auntie Ruth was going through a crisis and my presence was an extra strain, growing more critical with every day. I was sharpening my claws on my nearest and dearest, giving my belated rebellious puberty free rein. I was by now a crack debater, critical and dialectic, after years of interesting verbal disputes on home ground and I was beginning to conquer language as weapon. God help whomever crossed my path—I was always right. Even when I was proved, conclusively, to be wrong, I managed to rephrase the argument to *sound* right. Facts were not always important to me, I was flying toward the sun without wings, I could jump off high roofs without getting hurt. Sometimes. Not very often. Seldom. Only in dreams—still far from reality and my own life.

The day had come for the unavoidable confrontation. I presented my case. Papa vetoed it and that was that. He painted a secure future for me if and when I had learned feminine accomplishments and proposed that I should take a course in cooking immediately after school. I persevered with the theatre, he with cooking and "exciting recipes." He tried a new tack to the left with a career as kindergarten teacher. I remained stubborn. He suggested nursing "but the training is long and hard." I—actress. He—cookery and child care. And then he delivered the unkindest cut of all with crushing logic: "You are far too stubborn to ever submit to direction."

I don't know how and why it did, but that last argument really hit me hard. I believed him and saw ten years of dreams crushed and every escape route blocked, felt my body torn to pieces by wild inconsolable sorrow and disappointment, impossible to restrain. I reacted by pulling out all the stops, weeping and shaking and crying and howling, finally taking my refuge in the loo behind locked doors. Papa hammered on the door, alternating "let's talk about it" with "it's out of the question." I increased my noise volume every time he retracted, and eventually I had brought on a massive nosebleed. My first fearful thought was that my lungs had shattered and I opened the door to let papa see the horror he had caused. The blood gushed out and must have looked rather impressive. Papa paled visibly; he was not unfamiliar with that kind of sight. "It's only a nosebleed" he mumbled, impressed against his will and alarmed by my destructive bent. He telephoned the doctor and was advised to bring me to the accident clinic. The bleeding had almost stopped when we arrived at the hospital but I was utterly ravaged, couldn't still my tears, the crying reflexes quivering like fish under the eyelids and my whole body racked by sobs.

Papa wanted to reopen our discussion that evening, whereupon I declared that I would commit suicide if I was forced into domestic school and had I not "cooked meatballs for my father in his loneliness?" "They tasted like rubber" was Papa's truthful reply.

I refused to take part in further discussion, went to bed and couldn't sleep but started slowly to hatch a plan. Not a hope to go straight into acting, but maybe there was a possible detour. The three older children had been allowed to go to grammar school and Papa simply was not going to be able to deny me the same privilege. My plan was to attack through my stepmother. I felt that she wanted to be rid of me and would probably support my claim. I was going to propose that I would attempt to do in two years what the other three had done in four. It would be cheaper for one thing, and as an added attraction I would be spared four years of conventional schooling. I felt confident enough to try it; Papa had himself gone to a private crammer and with luck, my request might appeal to some tender memories. When I had passed my student examination, it was up to me to decide. Maybe I would be able to swing a loan to study. Maybe I could become an actress.

Early next morning, before anybody was up, I brought a big breakfast tray into the master bedroom. As soon as Papa had disappeared into the bathroom, I explained my plans to Auntie Ruth, who brightened perceptibly at the thought of my proposition. This was just, this was how it ought to be done. It occurred to me at first that her main object was to get rid of me but I soon realized that she, in her unmistakable loyalty to her own sex, truly rejoiced in my chances to achieve my goal. "Let the girl try" she said to papa and, O joy! papa hesistated . . . Auntie Ruth, whom I by now worshipped and adored, continued . . . "of course I'll do my bit. It goes without saying that I'll contribute economically so she can go to school and be properly taught. After all, her sister and brothers had their opportunity." Papa stopped protesting, he half-heartedly expressed a few pessimistic views but soon gave in and now we were all smiling. I promised to be good and diligent, I would share lodging with Tua and live cheaply, yes, I was willing to exist on bread and water if only they would let me go to Stockholm.

My sister and brothers expressed their doubt, they had no real faith in me, old prejudices die hard. To them I was a clown. I had to prove that I wasn't, this had become a matter of great importance to me. I wanted a proper *raison d'être*, respect, to be taken seriously. It was their mistake to think that I didn't exist because I did indeed exist. I was going to show them.

Stockholm! My first glimpse of the capital. The tram from the Central Station brought Tua and me to the very end of Karlbergsvägen, the part of it bordering the so-called "Nothing-forest." My memory is as vivid as if I were sitting in the shaking, badly lit tram at this very moment with the dense darkness of autumn outside and my imagination bursting with images of an immense tumultuous world with endless possibilities.

Our part of town was quite dreary, in fact, but to me it was as captivating as Rio de Janeiro, dangerous and alluring, full of life waiting just for me, ready to sink its teeth into me. My conception of The Big City was a blurred mixture of literary images where descriptions by Fridegård and Ahlin competed with local color drawn from the novels by Ivar Lo Johansson and Erik Asklund. Now it was my turn to act on that stage, to enter the dangerous world and find out if I measured up to the required standards.

The start was inauspicious. I curled up on the sofa in my room and stayed there, dreaming of The City outside. I felt scared and powerless in the anonymity of big city life.

Tua and I shared an old fashioned room with a porcelain stove, a small alcove for the hand basin and jug and three large bay windows. A window-seat was another refuge where I sat and looked out toward the Nothing-forest. Forests and trees always gave me a feeling of home, of belonging, in contrast to the town where I didn't feel at home. Across the street was our local grocery and next to it, the food factories of Norrmalm, constantly tempting us to no avail, with their most alluring smells. We had an arrangement to eat our main meals at the Margareta school, a crushingly boring boarding house, smelling of spinsters in aspic and prayer meetings with dill pickles. We soon tired of that establishment, bought an electric kettle and proceeded to cook interesting little rice dishes that had an unfortunate tendency to burn and made the tea taste of onions for months afterwards. Money was scarce but we had realized that it was possible to buy on tick when we had spent our respective monthly allowances. Papa was in for a surprise, eventually! Our circle of friends grew apace and I had inherited Mama's generosity together with her insistence on catering for the unknown guest and her "give and thou shalt receive thousandfold,"—only her prophetic words never seemed to come true.

Our landlady, Mrs. Persson, kept coming to our room to fill the water jug and close the damper on the stove while she droned on in her strange east coast dialect "you haave to cloose the daamper." We imitated her odd intonation and nasal twang and felt frozen to the marrow all the time due to the fact that the fire in the stove had a tendency to go out. All in all, it was a tough time, and as usual when threatened, or before I have adjusted to a new situation, I curled into a ball, playing possum in my lair.

Tua was my strong bastion and support. She was used to coping with life, strong and self-sufficient, the oldest child in a solid Swedish working-class family. She could deal with anything and was also a sensitive and loyal friend. I was too timid to use a telephone, found it difficult to handle practical matters, struggled ineffectively with bureaucracy, school registration and a thousand other trifling matters.

It wasn't that I had been spoiled, it was simply that I had never possessed a bank book or been entrusted with a comparatively large sum of money or learned how to order a meal in a restaurant and how to deal with people in authority.

I still don't cope too well with many of these practical problems but I have forced myself to realize that my inner helplessness and confusion don't show. What exposed me to the scorn of the world, however, was my unfortunate west-coast dialect. The entire population of Stockholm seemed hell-bent on letting me suffer for the way people in Gothenburg pronounce their vowels, and I had Kål and Åda and the harbor, the whole bloody Gothenburg thrown into my blushing and embarrassed face.

Tua. She wasn't exactly talkative, rather the opposite. With her slightly defective hearing, she often sat silent but very much waiting and watching. Sometimes she made up for her silences by talking nineteen to the dozen. She was beautiful, with large brown melancholy eyes, long fair hair and a thin mouth that now and again seemed to close on itself, as if to stop the words that were on the tip of her tongue. The dangerous revealing words. For my part, I didn't realize the danger, had no defense mechanism against people. If I started talking I didn't stop until I had revealed all. It is a beastly habit that has clobbered people, or in some cases induced them to deceive me and betray my unasked-for confidences. But thanks to my defenseless openness I have won my true friends.

Tua had two personalities, the quiet one, turned inward to poetry and dreams, wanting to be stroked. The other was competent and strong, went to drama school and could recite from *The Misunderstanding* by Camus in a voice already almost devoid of the Gothenburg drawl. In those days, drama students talked with long drawn-out open vowels. "To beeee or not to beeee . . . " In the evenings, when we were newly arrived, we used to sit, each in her own window-seat, and recite from the poetry of Karen Boye and Edith Södergran: "I looong for the laaand that does not exiiiist for aaaall that exiiists has no poooower to luuuure me." We sighed heavily and yearned for Him who would not only desire our bodies but our loving souls. He who would look into our real selves, deliver us and know the answers to all our intense longing, "in the month when laburnum and lilac are blooming."

I was a pupil at Enskilda Gymnasiet, a private crammer of the highest reputation. It was an expensive school and it was imperative that I study hard and pass my exams quickly, in the full knowledge that it was an economic sacrifice to keep me there.

Most of the students were the poor maladjusted children of wealthy parents, who were allowed to stay on at the school indefinitely, and indeed, indefinitely was the operative word. The school lacked exam privileges which meant that pupils had to pass their exams in eight mandatory subjects at other schools with unfamiliar teachers. Students who had chosen classical and modern languages instead of science subjects were expected to acquire some kind of competence in mathematics, geography and elementary physics and chemistry and pass a test in these subjects before embarking on the eight subjects of their choice.

I only had to start thinking about the final exam to feel a heavy ice cold stone inside me that would eventually explode into wild unreasoning fear, leaving me in a cold sweat with my stomach in cramps and a dry mouth. My only consolation was that the evil day was still in the far distant future.

The school had many incontrovertible advantages for its time, the beginning of the fifties. It was clearly unconventional. The headmaster was short, portly, temperamental and cheerful. Very occasionally, he would erupt in a sudden fit of temper that nobody seemed to mind. His staff was highly qualifed and it is still a mystery to me from where these, often elderly, gentlemen came and why they had chosen to teach in this place but one thing is certain: they were more interested in friendly, non-repressive instruction than in discipline. The school took a tolerant view of the general attitude of the students which meant less provocation during lessons and more genuine interest in the subjects. Pupils without incentive were allowed to go to sleep or simply to play hookey. Nobody was forced to attend, it was left to the individual.

Glorious freedom! No anxiety about school reports, no need to keep parents informed about progress; in fact, the pupils were graded only for their own information. Those who wanted it were shown a personal interest by the teachers, who were progressive, humorous and very kind to a man, and they all seemed to have graduated with honors in psychology, to make them ideal in dealing with a lot of highly strung individuals. To me, it was paradise. I devoured everything that took my fancy, stayed away from school when I felt like it and made up for my absence later as I was taught to be responsible for my own actions.

My Swedish teacher genuinely loved literature. He was an elderly, highly civilized gentleman who got so carried away when he recited Kjellgren that his face glowed with rapture and his deep voice shook with passion. It was pure joy to write essays when he allotted high marks for imagination and enthusiasm instead of minus marks for grammatical errors. I started to write essays in order to express my thoughts and feelings instead of suppressing them, my writing knew no bounds.

The English teacher had adopted English habits which made him a living illustration of an Englishman, a tea-drinking tennis player with liberal leanings. His gentle and ironic sarcasms were not directed against his pupils but gave a somewhat acid flavor to the meaningless stories about fox hunting and royalty that were included in the syllabus. He was like the very best aromatic bitter-orange marmalade.

The Latin teacher was a mysterious adventurer who used to be a sailor before he started teaching classical languages. My relationship with him was very personal and I was more than a little in love with him. He was a sensitive and clever teacher, a fairly unusual combination, as good pedagogues tend to develop a tough skin. Unfortunately, in spite of his excellence as a teacher and my crush on him, I was forced to sacrifice his subject.

There seemed to be no real choice. I had only two years to catch up on eight subjects and what's more, I ought to strive for good passes, so the logical conclusion was to sacrifice one, the Latin. I went to lessons and I studied and thoroughly learned to appreciate the poetry but my written work was more often than not unspeakably bad. My final written test is supposed to have surpassed all expectations. It had, according to legend, some literary qualities but no similarity whatsoever with the actual Latin text. My somewhat free interpretation had somebody straddling the back of a whale instead of crossing the Alps. I never did manage to reconcile myself to those dreary martial texts and military campaigns or to the pompous and inhumane orations that famous statesmen tended to spout, the foundation for our noble culture, rotten to the core.

The French teacher was a wit as well as being a robust sensualist and a gourmet. He quite often interrupted our grammar exercises to muse aloud about goodies in some well stocked patisserie before returning to the irregular verbs. I learned a lot of French in spite of the gastronomic excursions, or maybe it was thanks to them. You were gently and carefully stuffed with verbs—the knowledge had time to sink in and get absorbed like the best café filtre. He was a born storyteller with a store of fantastic, macabre tales, and another of his treats was to elevate each of the pupils in turn to the Personality of the Day, to be made much of for an hour or two. He had a warm heart and always dark shadows under his eyes.

Coexistence between the pupils could pose problems. Most of them were rich kids with expensive habits and arrogant manners, but that wasn't true of all of them. Quite a few were friendly enough and some were self-appointed, self-ironic clowns, always ready to amuse while they tried to prolong their childhood in order to keep at bay the unavoidable process of growing up.

From this group I acquired two faithful playmates, Andreas and Lou. Andreas died in an accident, otherwise we would still be playing together, but Lou and I have played tag and built sand castles for more than twenty years in the tough playgrounds of the big bad world, not seldom ending up as casualties with broken limbs and shattered nerves.

Some of the pupils came from the same vague middle-class background as I. We shared a sense of insecurity, nervous and scared that we wouldn't succeed, surrounding ourselves with barriers, the better to impress. The nobs had created the existing hierarchy at school by treating everybody outside their charmed circle as inferior transparent airbubbles.

There was among us the Scholarship Boy from the folk high school. He and I became friends, I think I was his only friend. The stigma of country speech brought us together. They laughed at me, immoderately and cruelly, the first day and for the next few weeks and after that they stopped taking any notice. Ove was not so lucky. He came from Holland and was a proletarian, that is, he considered himself a proletarian, dressed like one and expressed solidarity with the working classes although his background was not working class; his father was an esteemed and well known journalist. Ove had worked as a lumberjack for several years; he used to sit next to me and keep up a stream of talk during lessons that was completely unrelated to the subject taught. The teachers never tried to hinder him from talking and I had to train myself to concentrate on two different things simultaneously, absorb the teaching while I listened to him. Our relationship was secure and I mothered him to try to make him feel less frightened. The two of us shared a secret. He owned a jackknife and occasionally he would scratch my leg, just a very little, when nobody was looking. Our secret was that he possessed a Dangerous Weapon.

He was a highly intelligent, if eccentric, young man but he felt so unhappy among the upper-class pupils and with Stockholm in general that he simply was unable to apply himself to the process of learning. The teachers bent over backward in their efforts to support him but eventually he disappeared. Where did he go . . . ? Desperate and an outsider, he fell victim to the ruthlessness of privileged individuals. In this instance, the school was an example of society's uneven and unfair distribution of advantages.

What is it human beings expect from one another? Is it your duty to be at least slightly inferior to your fellows until the moment comes when they can use your strength? That is the time when they refuse to admit that you are only a weak vessel. Sometimes they expect you to to mirror their own image, to ratify their own existence. If you are then not affirmative enough, you are punished.

Punishment diminishes you and removes your confidence. You daren't open your mouth, cross the street, try to pass an exam. You allow others to control you and thereby confer on them the feeling of power they need to be able to suppress. It doesn't have to be complicated powergames:

Driving inspector: Mrs. Axelsson, are you allowed to drive when the light is red?
Myself (with trembling limbs and a buzzing head. No firm ground underfoot): Yes.

I have so far made three attempts to pass my driving test. I know how to drive and I know the rules and regulations by heart. What I cannot do is let myself be examined and judged. I have lived with the distinct suspicion for too long that some of my fellow creatures predict my incapability and feel "vindicated" every time I fail. I comply with their negative expectations or oblige with my own old insecurity.

I respond to people who expect me to succeed, I can feel them radiating positive attitudes, encouragement, kindness. The wish to ration the success of others is a common human failing. I am a human being and I sometimes feel impotent and envious when somebody else is too successful. I am aware of the dilemma, that's why I reason like this:

I would like to reach others without effort, without raising a circus tent and hoisting a trapeze every time. I want to be the stagehand who hoists the prima donna, myself, with a rope so high that she flies all the way up to heaven and stays there. Others have created that prima donna while I have tried to get out of playing the role for years.

What is it they expect of you? What do they want? You should always be sober but not averse to the odd drink. Avoid television except, of course, the good programs. Bake your bread with organically grown cereal. Demonstrate but not as a fanatic, be humane always but the same time fully aware of situations when violence is defensible. Shoes should be orthopedic, friendly to your feet. This view is not necessarily shared by shoe manufacturers and fashion designers. It's good for you to ski and jog and eat vegetables but it takes an awfully long time before you turn into a red beet or a turnip after death. You become good and straight and morally upstanding if you belong to all those associations that believe in "what is right." You ought to furnish your home with antique, stripped and Swedish pieces. Foreigners usually prefer brighter and shinier furniture but they are of course foreign and therefore underdeveloped. Women who believe in *what is proper* shouldn't really use makeup and their hair should be worn straight and emancipated.

Puritanism is a good old Swedish custom which people from abroad find difficult to acquire. Membership in the Association of Earth Shoe wearers assures you that you have done your bit to stop the end of the world: pollution, nuclear weapons, extortion and fascism can be avoided as long as you support what is right.

The month is April, the winter has been exceptionally harsh and one after the other, most of my friends have fallen into a black hole of depression. Everything around me is gray, including the dirty snow. I cling to my typewriter all day and cry in my sleep at night. I am paralyzed with fear but I can't allow myself the luxury to be depressed right now. I look at the same dreary landscape and follow the same dreary routine day after day. I listen to the footfalls of old age, relentlessly approaching. Funeral bells are tolling for dead cells, hair fine wrinkles and deep crevasses spring up everywhere, a mass of solid matter on the thighs, bad circulation. When I throw my head backward, I manage to look thirty, for a split second. If I am tempted to throw my head about, I get a crick in my neck, so I don't.

April, twenty three years ago, I sat in my furnished room in Stockholm and looked at a landscape with dirty snow and bare trees, longing to grow up and begin to live. I was ready to go but I must have missed the starting shot, was either too early or too late and, like the famous Japanese runner, headed for the forest where I found a flowering arbor suspended in my imagination— just above the ground. I stayed in my arbor most of the time, as I do now, dreaming. Except by now, reality has replaced fantasy. Or maybe I'm dreaming of my reality, of my imagined reality in my real imagination.

A lot of water has flowed under a lot of bridges in more than twenty years. I have experienced much that has been memorable, joyful and pleasing and horrid and painful. On balance I'm as insecure as I was then. Maybe in some respects I'm more confident, in others less; it probably evens itself out.

No longer do I erupt on the floor, stark naked and happy to

greet the new day, while my lover lovingly watches from the bed.

If there is somebody to share my bed, I'm very careful not to wake him when I slip out of the room in my dressing gown with the curtains drawn to protect me from a too unfriendly light and sit down alone—blissful moment—in the kitchen to enjoy a cup of poisonous, carcinogenic coffee while I think back on the previous night or all the days (and nights) gone by.

This doesn't necessarily mean that I take a negative attitude, that I don't want to look forward. I want to live and work, with respect for and interest in my fellow human beings toward a "solution" or relief from pain or regeneration and resurrection for crooked and straight alike. For the straight ones who meet a tangled life and believe it is open sea—and the twisted who meet open sea and see it as an overgrown jungle. I want to live and I want to work to the best of my ability.

Easter has been and gone again. That is the time when I always think of Greece and Greek Easter celebrations where theater is exemplified beautifully in the innermost sense of the word. Suffering and purification, katharsis and deus ex machina—the resurrection and the old priest in his long pale blue silk frock with a wooly scarf as protection against colds, taking shelter from the fireworks and hanging on for dear life to the precariously tottering pulpit outside church while the decorations of palm leaves are torn away by the strong wind from the sea, that also extinguishes all the candles—and the crowd singing *"Christós anesti"* with deafening force and shouting *"alithinos anesti."* Christ has risen, He has risen indeed!

One day Tua had had enough. She thought it was the outside of enough, the way I hid from the world, staying in night and day to read or to sleep. She was out a lot and when she came home, I was asleep.

Her first attempt was to drag me along one evening to a public lecture at the University. In those days, most lectures were restricted to bona fide students but this one was open to one and all. I can't remember the subject matter, only that there was a large crowd of people sitting on chairs in a vast hall. I had dressed to the nines, shaking with nerves, clammy hands, throat like sandpaper, high heels with my legs practically folding under me.

Tua had assured me that nothing could possibly harm me and that was perfectly true—the danger came instead from inside myself. Nobody made demands on me, nobody even looked at me, not much anyway—even if I tried to pretend that I attracted some attention. At first in Stockholm I was relieved to find that nobody seemed to take the slightest notice of anybody else; later I thought that I might as well be dead, judging from the complete lack of interest people seemed to take in one another. You simply didn't exist, unless you were married to somebody and even then it was doubtful if you existed.

The speaker started his lecture, the hall was quiet, you could have heard the proverbial pin drop and then another sound became evident, a quiet rhythmical rattling of a chair. It sounded as if somebody was making a noise on purpose, but it was certainly not on purpose that I was shaking uncontrollably from head to toe and the chair with me.

Tua gave me a worried glance and pointed toward the exit. We went to the loo and the shakes stopped. When we re-entered the hall, people did look. I sat down and after a few minutes I started shaking again: muscles contracting like shoals of fish weaving through the water. The spasms were beyond my control, I had to get up and leave, again, with Tua loyally bringing up the rear. Well outside, I couldn't stop crying, leaning against my coat in the cloakroom. I was inconsolable, everything came flooding in one rush, I didn't know why, was never going to know why.

The heat of spring was rolling in over Stockholm and we could keep our windows open. Tua was home more often and we used to sit looking longingly towards the Nothing forest. After the incident at the lecture, Tua stayed in or brought her friends home for me to get to know: exciting and dramatic people with beautiful diction, they excelled in long drawn out open vowels.

I was busy that spring term, preparing for my exam in German, both written and oral. I felt less insecure at school with Lou and Andreas; we still laughed a lot together. Lou introduced me to her friends and invited me to her home, where I could laugh with her friends too. Laughter at the slightest provocation, as some kind of ritual or unconscious therapy. I must have given the impression of an unusually gay dog or, at least, somebody who was easily amused. A pleasant and easy-going light weight affair started at a party chez Lou. I laughed away the night with a young law student but the affair didn't last long.

Sometimes I remembered Manne. Memory of Manne "Maybe, Manne, Memory." . . . that's how one of Tua's fellow students might have expressed it. But Manne had no memory of me. With him I had felt mature and almost grown-up, he had accepted me. Now I was back in my well-known feeling of unreality.

But what is reality? What is more real for somebody who is unreal than her unreality? What would we do without our dreams? When does hope fade? I still can't distinguish the borders between different foreign countries in my dream world. I lacked the necessary visas: for reality, that is, objective reality, and also for entry into the world of grown-ups.

Tua declared one evening that the time had come for my next departure into danger. We were going to "Prinsen," a dangerous restaurant full of dangerous people.

We had previously been out together at the "Guldtuppen" on St. Eriksgatan where we had eaten steak with pommes frites and garlic butter. Consulting my memory, that must have been the first time I ever tasted pommes frites and garlic butter. It was only the two of us and no danger was involved, I looked neither right nor left, nowhere but at my plate and gave myself up to sheer enjoyment.

What madeleine cakes meant to Proust in his childhood corresponds exactly to what pommes frites and garlic butter meant to me. Who can understand that?

Many chips and a lot of garlic butter have passed through my alimentary canal without bringing me back each time to that particular phase of adolescence, but at this moment, the taste of unspoiled chips and a virgin mound of butter bring back, with unexpected force, the frightening and wonderful time.

Slowly I squeezed myself into the world, out of the womb into a bigger space. I was wont to retrace my passage back to security and protective darkness, only to force an exit again with one shoulder foremost and my head smeared with blood. Rebirth upon rebirth.

We were heading for "Prinsen," the chips and the garlic butter. The restaurant was supposed to be a favorite meeting place for interesting people and artists, the sort of people I had met in Gothenburg at least once or twice but now I felt as if I had never met one single human being before, as if I hailed from the wide open spaces in the North, from the deserted countryside. I was different, I had no past. How can that be explained?

Can environment really mean that much? Is that one reason why old people die on leaving the home they have lived in for the last forty years to go to a place in the suburbs? Is that why you melt into the background and become nothing more than a shadow against the wall, lost like a survivor of a nuclear explosion that destroyed everything around you? The umbilical cord spells security, that is how it seems, anyway.

The eighteen years I had lived were obliterated, I felt like a fish thrown up on the beach until I slowly started to develop legs and begin walking. We humans experience the same slow conception and evolution again and again, ourselves containing the whole universe and the entire course of history.

"Prinsen" was crammed with people and many of them knew Tua, even I had met a few. They were friendly enough. An Indian started drawing my portrait, an actor pronounced that I was a potential "lion" and was destined to be, if I only dared, a *real* lion. He said that I was strong.

That was the moment when I felt the first tremors, they multiplied like rabbits and mice and soon I was shaking like a leaf, my stomach contracting painfully as I strained to control reactions. Tua tried to cure my ills with large doses of wine, a cure that not only didn't help but sent me to the loo where I stayed locked in until a crowd of desperate females started hammering on the door. Forced to leave this safe haven, I dragged myself back to the table like an old woman condemned to death, still shaking. Tua wasn't going to let me escape; more wine was poured into me but the shakes continued until I was more than half drunk. Then, suddenly, I was on top of the world, allowed the Indian to use me as a model and started feeling like a *real* lion.

Tua and I each went home with a boyfriend that night. What happened afterwards has left no memories; several months of my life are veiled in darkness. Was all this due to pommes frites and garlic butter? That's unlikely. Why would these culinary treats mean that much to me? I had, after all, eaten lots of chips in Paris at the age of fifteen. "Prinsen?" I often went there afterward without shaking; also without memories. The shakes were buried underneath—waiting for the next disembarcation, the next stretch of unknown coast and new cannibals.

After my first year in Stockholm, I divided my summer vacation between home and my sister's. I had passed my A-level German with an A minus grade but nobody at home paid much attention. I had also managed to clear the hurdles of O-level passes in maths and geography, maybe not a great deal to brag about but to me it represented a great feat. I had conquered a fraction of an inch of self-confidence, which gave me the impetus to struggle on.

Together with two other pupils, I had three weeks of private tuition with a kindly and understanding maths teacher. I don't remember that I understood any of the complicated root systems he used to rave about, but when the time had come for me to sit the test in a strange and unfamiliar school under the eyes of another benevolent teacher, I seemed to take dictation from above and achieved a pass. I had passed, passed *the maths*—without knowing in the least how.

It was soon time to return to Stockholm and it couldn't be too soon for me. Gothenburg seemed like a small provincial town and I behaved as if one and all in it were country bumpkins speaking in an incomprehensible dialect while I did my artificial best to mimic Stockholm speech, to the huge enjoyment of my two brothers.

Tua and I had the whole empty summer town to wander in, and the anxiety I had used to feel in Stockholm was gone with the wind, at least for the moment. I had no sudden attacks of nerves, no shakes.

One rare beautiful afternoon in August when we were walking in the town center, a car drove up and stopped Tua. My fate sat in that car. I met somebody who would radically change my whole life. Tua's friend drove the car and Lasse was the passenger, he who was going to become my "fiancé" and I his "femme unique," for the next three years his one and only, unique, unequalled, matchless woman, whom he would try to love madly, with *amour fou.*

Lasse is a poet, an exceptional person with his head full of wonderful and extraordinary images, ideas and thoughts that he sometimes could and sometimes couldn't or didn't want to write down.

Lasse stepped out of the car and he seemed to carry the heavens on his shoulders, he was that tall—his image-laden brow shot up among the summer clouds.

My insecurity has always been boundless, I was born with it and it is likely to stay with me till I die. I carry it with me in my rucksack always, nobody wants it and I can hardly bear it myself. In the same rucksack I carry what's left of my umbilical cord, pathetic as a dried-up piece of algae. Now and then it revives. Watch out! It is searching for its lost stump, its continuity, its flow of blood, its property.

The dried-up cord changed into a snake full of pulsating life, left my rucksack and soundlessly found a new home within Lasse.

I fell in love on the spot, full of *amour fou* indeed, and my admiration for his knowledge, wit and poetical imagery knew no bounds. After the first couple of hours that we spent at a restaurant, "Kometen," I was completely lost or maybe resurrected is a better word, as our relationship was going to develop me and give direction to my life. Lasse was the intermediary, and as such, remarkably generous.

In later years I have often thought how rare it is to find men who have already covered some distance of the way willing to give a helping hand to a woman at the start of her career. I have found support on a few occasions, but more often active attempts to stop and suppress me, shut me up. I never had much of a chance, when I think back, to work on an equal footing with men. There always seemed to be a considerable difference in the judging of male versus female art and talent. Man supposedly possessed thought and knowledge and woman was given credit for a twice-exposed, pathetic and magnified feeling as compensation for her inability to think. At least, that's how critics and others seem to reason. Prejudices are still buried deep and firm under the smooth surface, hanging on with sharp and anxious teeth to men and women alike.

I wrote a book about Greece during the junta, using a male pseudonym. A couple I knew quite well, recommended it warmly until they were told that the book was written by a woman. Then they abruptly stopped praising what had previously found favor with them, crestfallen by their mistake.

We had barely left the restaurant when this celestial tower bent toward me with great tenderness and cradled me with a warmth that I had always been longing for. I lost sight of the ground, forgot the mud on my shoes and floated heavenward into the infinite world of poetry.

We spent our first night together in my childhood home, made love in the bed where I had suffered so much anguish, and through the night I kept running to the window, expecting a punishing thunderbolt to strike. Catastrophe seemed to be a logical consequence of such an earth-shaking experience.

My parents were expected home but not until the next day. I felt insecure in this environment with Lasse, I don't know why. Maybe our poetic meeting shouldn't have taken place in a house so filled with sorrow and bitter, hurtful memories.

Memory tends to draw a veil across the most important events of one's life only to let them be dimly seen as fragments. Was the end of the affair so bitter to me that I have obliterated what ought to have been the first happy memories? Or was our life together so rich and real, self-contained and finished that it doesn't lend itself to nostalgic rediscovery, reproduction, desecration? When separation loomed, I tried to dull the pain by tearing holes in the lovely myths surrounding our relationship. That was the only way I could continue existing, after The Treachery.

Autumn. We spent some time with Lasse's parents in the Stockholm archipelago. The islands are well-wooded, dark and dangerous, very different from the dazzling openness I had experienced in Bohuslän. I felt like a stranger. Lasse's parents were cultivated and amiable—but I didn't belong, not in their home, not on the little island. I wanted to know exactly where I was with Lasse. Was it true that we were a couple, as he claimed—or was that nothing but fiction and dreams? His wish for complete freedom hurt me from the start. I wanted ties, firm and forever. Security and belonging for ever and ever.

Lasse wrote letters to me from the island, beautiful serious letters that impressed me deeply and increased my infatuation and, at the same time, my uneasiness. In spite of his tenderness, his slender fair body, his tremendous poems and words, Lasse wasn't unlike the islands where the water is dark and opaque; where tall fir trees throw long shadows on the still water; where you can't see the bottom of the sea which makes it dangerous; where strange birds cry in the night like evil harbingers of sorrow.

"I am sitting on the step, the sun is pouring out its light and I hope to sail over to X with this letter. The summer is big and blue and stretches for ever but when one is alone, it becomes sad. It is fabulous to make love in the summer, especially on an island. That's why I would love for you to come and play with me. But if you're starting school it can only be for the weekend and that's too short, isn't it?"

Lasse wrote.

I could have robbed a bank, gone to Tierra del Fuego if he had asked me, even for a day, done anything. To be together, to share everything: the dreams and the reality.

Lasse had a streak of practicality among his visions and surreallistic images, an attribute he shares with most men. They may walk around like the hero in *The Fantastic Tales of Baron Münchausen*, with flowers growing in their hair, a passionate longing for other worlds, a strong belief in ideas and their divine truths and an honest ambition to solve the mysteries of life, but they are perfectly capable of protecting their feet with gumboots, picking their noses, figuring their bank balances, scolding their editors and planning imaginary affairs with great actresses or entertainers, who will be impressed by their rare genius. A man, like most men, is careful to maintain his affair with his current bedmate in good order; he wraps her in a poetic, extravagantly decorated, flamboyant, homespun blanket, a warming blanket. One day the blanket slips and the companion dies of exposure. The poet gives her a life she didn't have before, shows her another identity than the one she knew.

I absorbed everything and I developed because I was spared the role of passive muse but could take part instead in creative enthusiasm and its mysteries, in the writing of poetry, in the learning of topics outside the school curriculum, in a brave new world of thoughts and ideas that were bound to rearrange the whole substance of my life.

Lasse brought me into his literary world as a matter of course. And why not, I ask myself today. But the suppression of women was heavier then, like a heavy weight on my thoughts and opinions. My fate could have been worse, I might have been sat on instead of liberated.

Lasse took an interest in my writing, encouraged me and praised my efforts. It was a genuine interest, not from above and protective but in a natural and self-evident manner as if I were his twin, a sibling, not to compete with but to give a friendly push in the right direction. Besides, I was also able to contribute some knowledge that he could benefit from. He had, after all, left school very early.

All of Lasse's colleagues weren't equally generous. They made a point of noticing me, even accepting me, because I was Lasse's bird, but they had absolute confidence in their own superiority and their brand new academic degrees. They seemed to think that they were automatically qualified to step into the old patriarchal shoes, and the spirit of the jackboot was hovering over me as well as over their own female companions.

There were a few honorable exceptions but the general consensus was that females didn't amount to much. Only men could aspire to become poets, and then Sappho—but she was long dead and besides, a lesbian. Karin Boye was ridiculous and commonplace and Edith Södergran was sentimental, they said. It was remotely possible that their poetry had some literary value, that value mainly acquired through "reassessing" academic dissertations.

We played poetic games in the beginning of our love affair. You are supposed to answer abstract questions, not knowing the questions, with poetic definitions. The resulting images can have a wide range, from softly floating to abrasive, from dizzyingly light to penetratingly heavy wallows. Before I started playing word games I had been influenced by Boye and Södergran but I had also written poems in a rather personal style influenced by the unsentimental, salty and burlesque language of my two brothers.

I tried writing in the severe and plain French manner, too, like some of the older poets I had studied in Paris, using traditional meter and rhymes. I managed to produce lines in French that looked truly impressive, although translated into Swedish they were nothing but dust. I described my tired blood, my ennui and the transience of life. I was more weary than all the fin-de-siècle poets rolled into one and I sometimes impressed even myself with my new-found sophistication.

Through Lasse, I became strongly influenced by French and Spanish surrealists, but first and foremost by his own poetry that was influenced by those same poets. Images always *become* your own like absinthe poured in a milk bottle. Lasse was bound to his native Sweden by close ties. He was and is a master in the art of translating French images into Swedish reality. After some time in the company of Lasse and his fellow poets, my poems started to look like this:

> Oh, boundless spaces, open your morbid holes in the ice
> and let out the imprisoned girl with her glowing hair
> let her whirl and swirl like a cloud of pollen

let her fingers guard all foolish paper shepherds
with muddled letters.
Let her immerse her white thighs into the lung of the moon.
When the white plague has added up figures in our corridors
neither the seagull nor the chimney sweep, with his hot
    plummet, smile.
When the white plague with its growling throat has tuned all
tight drums,
there will be neither a baton beating time towards a magical
twilight
nor an indifferent handkerchief waving in the navel of
the train.
Then is the time for the grass to drag its thin skin out
towards the sea
and let waterlilies hide their bloom in the mud.
Then is the time for man to step down into the teeming
earth
and mould himself a dress-coat, sharper than the mirror
    glass, colder than the stranger.
And we will observe through our double microscopes
how amoebas, dressing up in floor length mantles
and with painted eyepupils, set out on their endless
migration towards the extinct age-old volcanoes.

I felt that Paul Andersson was an intimate friend the first time we met. We could laugh together and I felt that he accepted me without reservations. "Paul of Pauper," he used to say, "is a formal expression for hunger that is now replaced by the word poor." He was a deliverer, he dared to look deep, to shoulder the burden of hell and tormented suffering. He went in search of an artificial paradise, a mystic without academic schooling but with the fresh and spontaneous knowledge of the self-taught. He had placed himself outside all competition of his own free will, an outsider already at birth who questioned everything that others accept, either from blindness or sheer habit. His poetry suspended the laws of gravity and he fell silent in order to live in his own glowingly fantastic and corrosive world. He shared his skin and gave away his eyes and he never closed his mouth like a miser to grudge joy to others. Being generous to a fault, he gave away his life bit by bit and ultimately received it back—he was, after all, a mystic—by sharing his spirit among many of his fellow human beings.

Lasse was an auto-didact as well, but he lacked Paul's courage to be an outsider in his life as in his writing, that had earned him a name as a Swedish Rimbaud. Lasse lived in a state of unrelieved tension that hindered him in expressing his wealth of images. He is more gifted and dynamic than most poets but he often lacked the self-confidence needed to bring it out. The result has been that others have taken advantage of him or that he has withdrawn or remained silent until the pressure within him has caused an explosion; a new collection of poetry or poetry translation or any other poetical activity meant to strike a blow for the glory of poetry. Poetry as the only alternative to darkness. Poetry as despair. Poetry as joy.

Quite a few writers surrounded him in those days, some of whom later elbowed him aside on their road to glory. Stubborn, clever climbers who had been been pursuing their goal since childhood, to enter the Swedish Academy one day. Able poets, who knew what they were about, knew their lesson by heart, had chosen the correct middle road, the correct properly sanctioned protests and the correctly balanced pathos whatever cause was at stake. They possessed an unmistakable talent for recognizing current trends, sometimes riding with the trend, at other times pretending to go against it to show the right amount of rebelliousness. It goes without saying that they knew how to get along with the pundits, the influential ones. They were admirably talented for prostitution, for licking the arses of those who had sweet rewards in their power, and they knew how to turn their backs on those who are at the bottom of the ladder.

Lasse wrote a lot but published very little, as I did. Both of us lacked confidence, we alternated between self assertion and repressive shyness; we read our poems, stuttering and with flaming cheeks, to small audiences and stumbled along warily in the dangerous world just to surprise our public on unexpected occasions with sudden flashes of inspiration that literally left them breathless. The whole world was ours in sudden mad moments.

A literary magazine *Upptakt* started with Lasse as one of the editors. There I had my first poems rejected, but they published my translation of Paul Celan's *Todesfuge*. In this translation I collaborated with the exotic bird of passage and faithful friend through the years, Pierre Zekeli with whom one never converses in less than seven languages—although he's master of many more than that.

I met Tomas Tranströmmer and my poems acquired the symbol of a seagull. Tomas was straight and honest, I felt strongly drawn to him but he kept an inner distance, he seemed to stretch out one hand to say "come closer" while he guarded himself with the other. I believe that is how many feel in relation to me: I have two different personalities, one part of me can be approached and loved without any danger involved, the other is ready to attack, armed to the teeth. My weapons are mostly directed towards myself, however, and my bark is considerably worse than my bite.

I met many poets. Many of them turned out to be faithful friends and others pretended to be while they deceived me time and time again; and still others simply preferred to shut their eyes when they passed me by.

It was a wild time when you could hold the rain off by shouting "sun" and you only had to lift the clouds to get a better light.

Already, in Gothenburg, I had found my political creed through films, books and the people I had met.

I didn't know enough and couldn't pretend to have a competent knowledge about the state of the world, but Lasse taught me much during our time together, mostly about international conditions, and he also prompted me to delve deeper in this sphere.

One day, coming out from the cinema, Lasse stopped in front of a tall, powerfully built man and they greeted one another. The wife of this walking tree kept in his shadow. Like a small vixen, a silky lynx, she peeped out, pricking up her ears. Maria Wine, Artur Lundkvist: famous people, dangerous people. My immediate instinct told me, as usual, to run away and hide.

The writer Artur Lundkvist was father of a kind to Lasse, father as teacher and friend, somebody who radiated firm good sense. I knew that Lasse looked up to him. I was confused, attracted and repelled at the same time by his forceful personality, so very like Papa's. His uncompromising attitude frightened me, his candor and openness were wont to provoke promising argument, but I could sense an invisible clenched fist in the background. My first impression was of a man with strong feelings, lively imagination and solid strength, strength that could be both good and dangerous. Later I saw other things: the poet, sensitive and pure of heart, the dreamer who ceaselessly worked to reveal social injustice, the ills of our time, the ravages of violence and suppression in a world that Lasse and I, as yet, knew little about.

My first quick and impatient attempt to draw Artur and Maria presents a picture that has since changed and deepened with the years. New issue has regularly sprung out of this fruitful dialectic and spirited relationship. Maria Wine's sensitive but valiant woman's poetry has inspired me. Her pliancy hand in hand with strength made sense to me in my own divided world, gave me courage to use images as she did, from within, brave and timid, feminine and anonymous at the same time.

From Karlbergsvägen to Kungsholmen and Mrs. Fast-berg's three-roomed flat. She was a big handsome woman with an old fashioned thick knot of hair and penetrating eyes. She gave me a guided tour round the flat as if it had been a castle. "And this is the kitchen" she said in the accents of somebody announc-ing "and this is the Taj Mahal." The kitchen was large and she demonstrated all the nooks and crannies, secret places, cup-boards and drawers. I couldn't quite understand why she went into all these details, I had after all only advertised for a room. During the tour of inspection she kept her beady eye on me. Would the answer be yes or no? The whole thing was clearly a rit-ual to test all applicants before she made up her mind as to their trustworthiness. That was good common sense, as she intended to leave the flat to the mercy and sole occupation of her lodger for a longer period—while she went away. That is how I acquired a flat of my own although I really only made use of the bedroom, kitchen and bathroom. My landlady had left so much of her im-print on the flat that she was almost there in body. She seemed to sit on top of her crowded pile of furniture, busy crocheting some new bedspread.

It suited Lasse and me to have our own flat, only Lasse never got used to the place, he thought it was ugly and strange. I was touched by my landlady's trust in me and rather liked living there. It was the very first time I had had a home of my own and it made me feel almost independent.

I was back at school, setting off each morning, maybe not quite as diligently as the previous year; but eventually I found a con-venient routine that also allowed me to stay at home now and again to play poetic games.

I also played the role of the little housewife, shopping and cooking. I liked this role because it was new, and ignorant as I was, I didn't realize that this was the first step of what was going to be a murderously boring routine.

While I went to school, Lasse drifted round Stockholm, visited bookshops and sat writing in noisy cafes. Sometimes he spent hours lying on the bed, singing Rodgers and Hart with a romantic empathy that melted my heart. He had copied the song texts in a notebook and every line seemed to be directed at me: "I see your face in every flower . . ." That was my face he was singing about. I felt completely enveloped by delicious sentimentality; wallowing in thick layers of schmaltz and sweet dreams. Never mind the influence of great and admired men of letters like Breton, Eluard and Lorca, never mind tragedies in the real world, Franco and Marx.

These were years when the blue moon shone, "Night and Day" sent pleasurable shivers up my back and the saxophones from the nearest ballroom sounded like Harlem itself.

By this time I was beginning to count on Lasse's presence for all eternity and I felt secure in that knowledge. That was his cue for announcing his forthcoming trip to Paris and Spain, imperative to him and a terrible blow to my deep infatuation. He assured me that I was to follow him as soon as I had passed my exam and further that we belonged together, also that the projected journey was of great importance to his development as writer and artist. I started to hate school. Lasse planned to leave in January and I had to find another place to live as Mrs. Fastberg was returning from Malmö with her new husband.

The state of my new lodgings served to distract my initial feelings of sorrow and loss. I had found a room in a turbulent home on Mosebackstorg, where the widow of an army officer had six paying guests, one daughter who was a pop singer with a live-in fiancé, another daughter my age, dogs and various other small animals. This was a foretaste of latter-day hippie communes with an atmosphere of madness and freedom. The vibrations were good but hardly conducive to studying. The family was middle-class at heart and the state of affairs was humiliating for them.

They made it clear that if the master of the house had been alive, there would have been no necessity to take in paying guests. I sympathize with their problems. It must have been sheer hell with all these people. The two daughters and their "fiancés" made their presence strongly felt with song and laughter, cosmetics and alcohol and clothing everywhere. It was all very festive and exciting, with kissing and quarrelling in each corner, but in the long run it was a great strain. I couldn't keep my clothes and other belongings as somebody or other always "borrowed" them and forgot to return them and I wasn't exactly rolling in money myself. My one and only winter coat disappeared and so did I, finally. That calamity was the last straw as by then I had nothing warm to wear. The younger daughter had a lot of problems that kept both of us up through the nights, trying to solve them. There wasn't much time left for homework after that drink with one of the "fiancés" and taking the dogs for their walk. The widow was kind and warm-hearted to the extent that she would have opened her already overflowing home to a further six needy lodgers—whether they could pay their rent or not. She was very much like Mama in her self-effacing generosity.

I moved from Söder to Gärdet and Mrs Stagnelius. By now I have lived in all the different parts of Stockholm and since 1958 exclusively in Söder (the South Bank).

Mrs Stagnelius was old and handicapped, strikingly intelligent and well-read and I enjoyed her company very much. She had one daughter, who was all the world to her and who visited her occasionally. The daughter was a good-looking woman who could have stepped out of a play by Hjalmar Söderberg. What Söderberg didn't know about women gave them an extra secretive dimension, an almost unknowable quality. She was dark and interesting, full of female secrets, plagueing her and tearing her to pieces, and her passionate face bore tell-tale traces.

Mrs Stagnelius was left on her own most of the time and seemed to like that. She sometimes invited me to tea and polite conversation; on these occasions all the niceties were observed:

the antique tea service, the cakes and the elegant literary conversation that often touched upon the Great Poet, long since dead although the name lived on. Naturally his name was not Stagnelius.

I had a very small room, the maid's room next to the kitchen. By now I was famliar with that kind of room where there is only space enough for a bed, under which all one's belongings have to go.

My window was large, facing the open Gärdet, formerly an army exercise field. I sat on my bed in the little room, lonely as in a well, and stared at life, waiting for me on the outside. I watched the sun set every night, far away on the tall red brick buildings, and linger on the windows, behind which unknown people lived their unknown lives. The windowpanes glowed like thousands of blind mirrors, unfathomably. Impenetrably the glass reflected the bright sunshine until my eyes hurt, my breast hurt. I could sit for hours and watch the sunsets, and the memory of them has followed me through the years. I can't explain why I feel upset and oppressed by the memory and at the same time how I long for something I can't identify . . . . It's nothing to do with the beauty of the spectacle, it's rather the epitome of universal forsakenness and longing. Everything was hidden in the glowing windows and the red bricks darkening against the deep blue sky of a March twilight. That belonged to another world, to a dream of another life than mine.

It was a time of desperation because now I was beginning to miss Lasse, all of him, his muscles and sinews, his bone structure, teeth, his nails and even the dirt under the nails. His mouth and tongue, his male member that ought to have its rightful place inside me and his cocky laughter and his humble tenderness. I missed him so intensely that I was in danger of disappearing.

He personified the Big Hunger and the Deep Thirst that nobody can slake. The need for love, for consolation that you drag behind you like a threadbare trawl through life.

I suffered from acute stomach pains, my ability to study diminished and the dreaded exam loomed closer and closer. It was soon two years since I had left Gothenburg.

Lasse sent me a postcard when he reached Paris, telling me all was well; after that nothing. I phoned his parents who tried to calm me by their assurances that he never ever wrote letters. But he had promised and I had believed him. I waited and suffered and the kind Mrs Stagnelius sympathized. After one month, I sent an express letter, and after two more weeks of silence—a telegram. Then I had a message from a friend of a friend that I shouldn't send express letters, they were delivered much too early in the morning and woke everybody up.

I was going out of my mind, lost more than twenty pounds in a few weeks and looked gaunt and haggard. My landlady guessed of course what was going on, my bitter crying must have disturbed her through many long nights. She took to inviting me more frequently and tried bravely to distract my thoughts.

That is how she came to introduce the recurrent Sunday lunches, the same, never-to-be-forgotten dish on each successive Sunday. The poor old tired Mrs Stagnelius put two slices of white bread to soak in milk on Saturday night; on Sunday morning she dipped them in bread crumbs and fried them. When she had squeezed the bread with her old hands that she never washed, much too much trouble washing, the bread was gray and her hands a little cleaner. Fried bacon and eggs topped the fried bread; it looked terrible but tasted fine. I tried at first to get out of accepting the invitations but grew accustomed and learned to love those dirty, lovingly prepared slices of bread that she firmly insisted on preparing with her own hands.

My gloomy state of mind became, if possible, gloomier still. I absent-mindedly helped Mrs Stagnelius get into and out of the bath tub every two or three weeks, while my thoughts were firmly fixed on Lasse in Paris, every step he took, every person he met, every girl he slept with, every poem he wrote that I couldn't read.

Spring was around the corner, implacably cruel. Tomas came to see me, very occasionally, and took me out, very properly. I met friends while my tired and ailing soul stubbornly hovered over Paris, in some cafe where I imagined Lasse to sit. I refused to believe that he had abandoned me, that our affaire was over. I was his one and only love, wasn't I? "La femme unique." Or maybe I wasn't? Maybe that was something nobody could aspire to be. Maybe it was just me, as usual, unforgivably naive and full of false hope.

April came and I studied as in a dream or trance. The exams were upon me and I passed all the written tests apart from the Latin, as expected. Nothing mattered to me but a letter that wouldn't arrive, that was my sole preoccupation.

One day it came. *The Letter*. The letter that contained all I had ever hoped for—albeit five months too late. It said "forgive me" and "the sad Paris where you always want to die and everybody wastes your time." And he continued, as if nothing untoward had happened, as if we had made love the night before and he had only gone away for the day—"we ought to get married" and further on he mentioned that I should pack some tinned food because he was penniless and hungry and waiting for me. He loved me!

My joy knew no bounds. I was the richest of the rich and needed nobody else. Mrs Stangelius turned into a lonely pauper overnight. Our Sunday lunches came to an end. I started going out and I studied and I met people and I amused myself because now I *knew*. My silly conceit floated like a bunch of balloons over my head, and behaving like a cocky five-year-old, I didn't even notice when I became airborne and was carried away—all because of a letter—for a few words—for the sake of a few dreams. Away from reality, up above the rooftops away from school and exams . . . toward Paris.

More letters followed the first, warm as well as practical. Lasse needed me in different ways. He wrote sensible, intelligent and poetical letters that proved his superior knowledge and made me shiver with inferiority and also prompted me to memorize the name of every single writer and artist he mentioned. I was hardly fit for normal life, I only lived for the moment when I would meet him again. I was going to Paris, if I had to walk all the way, yes, preferably on foot or maybe crawling on my hands and knees so that I could prove my unsurpassed love. Bleeding, crawling and trod-on—evidence of immeasurable love in a tormented soul. Lasse's silence hadn't increased my love, rather the opposite, although I was not prepared to admit it. His silence had awakened my masochistic tendencies and weakened my confidence.

Part of my love floated with the balloons high above the rooftops; another part rested in a grave.

When you are firmly convinced that you mean nothing to the one person, this destructive belief becomes the driving force behind your efforts to achieve importance and rehabilitation, but since this force is sick and masochistic, it increases your insecurity and anxiety and it makes you shy of love and the object of your love. Your lover doesn't really care as long as you make yourself useful in your devotions; it is practical and handy to have somebody who worships and is willing to perform little services for the vicarious pleasures they give. It is splendid to have somebody in attendence who doesn't know her worth or is not burdened by too much self-confidence, somebody who waits and exists on preset conditions, who is forgettable and undemanding. Somebody who won't give her lover up but is willing to give and give of herself.

I devoured every word in Lasse's letter. I underlined and placed them next to my heart, knew them by heart. I almost burst with gratitude when it said at the bottom "I kiss you" after all the descriptions of exhibitions, planned books, practical problems and fine poetical passages. From the poetry I received nourishment, it gave me a sense of identity and self-assurance in spite of my masochistic efforts in self-negation. Somehow the poet within me felt equal to Lasse the poet, and refused to be repressed. A part of the unconscious self that won't be subdued, your unalienable right to speak and think according to the demands of conscience, not of society. Everybody possesses this free zone in spite of all indoctrination, branding and impressing. You owe it to yourself to listen to its voice!

Lasse experienced a snowbound Sweden from his vantage

point of Paris in spring and he made me long for fresh snowfalls so that I would be able to express my *own* poetical experience of my *own* snow in my *own* country. Listen to the words of the poet:

I constantly long for a possible winter when I am away from home. I want to write about the Swede abroad, about the Swede who carries his winter inside, his winter that is greater and prouder than any other season. He exhales magnificent frosty breaths under a sun that ploughs and ploughs, drawn by a monotonous cloud. He takes a snow step right through the curtain and the foreign city catches him and embraces his wintry soul, his blond thought. The Swede makes love to a whore, wrapped in wallpaper, he seals their union with a winter's kiss. They create a poetic snowfall for a brief moment and afterwards he dreams, unhappy and melancholy as a bear, about her olive hued breasts under the mediterranean moon. That's why we have all our sea shanties.

It was May in Paris and Lasse was still dreaming of his Swedish winter.

They've found a name for books like this: "Confessional literature"— as long as they are written by women. I think the term is
pretty bloody awful and it has a sickly religious slant, although I
suppose it has its uses. Men have been writing books about themselves since the ark but their books are classified as "autobiog-
raphy" or having an "autobiographical character," depending
on how well or badly the author has camouflaged whatever he
wanted and needed to get to grips with: himself.

Most of the writers I know have written "confessional" books. I
have been a slow starter. I have been working on this book, more
or less deliberately, during the last ten years, although originally
it was meant to deal with Sweden. I used to think that it was Sweden only that was heading in the wrong direction. At this moment, when I have finally managed to get going on the book
(maybe it is the first of several) that is supposed to show what is inside the egg, what makes a person develop this rather than that
way, show how it is to hatch and grow, yes, at this very moment
quite a few writers who share my need have been forced into the
cramped quarters of "confessional literature" where we sit and
squeal like mice, in a lump. The same books written by men
would have been called something different, something more
precise, something able to open wider and more meaningful perspectives of the world. Men *are born* meaningful and able to grap-
ple with great problems when they're in nappies. They imbibe
deep true meaning and historical dialectics with their little
mouths, sucking Mother Earth's nipple and receiving the Truth
together with their mother's milk.

Little girls pick fleas out of each others fur and eat them, after
having carefully examined the tiny creatures—as do chimpan-

zees and monkeys—when they aren't playing with dolls or ba-
nanas.

A *terminology* gives you the right to deal with anything and
everything: with human beings, their striving and their achievement.

For many it is essential to sort through life, wrap and pack and
label it or, if you are a writer, maybe hand out small portions of
what you "have attained" to your readers.

I scoop straight out of my amniotic fluid, I rip open my shirt as
the lover, mad with love, bares his breast to convince of the
depth of his feelings. I can't present my work in tidy periods, I'm
hit by lightning, suddenly and brutally hit by blinding insight
and between the flashes there are long silences.

Value judgments, uttered by male critics on women's literature, are almost without exception self-generating, ready formu-
lae:

"In her book *The Clouds Are Singing* she has formulated a phi-
losophical, pantheistic view of life that deepens background and
content of her earlier rambles and casual excursions in the spiritual sphere."

Or: "With her book *I Want To Conquer You, Fire* she has openly professed herself an adherent to the expressionistic life experience that caracterizes D. H. Lawrence but she has added her
own unmistakably feminine and emotional stamp that distin-
guishes her earlier books, where the seething content exquisitely
complements the male reasoning and intellectually logical prose.
To use a daring image, you could say that the female prose is firm
and solid like the earth *underneath* the clouds floating above in
airy abstract formation."

Or; "In her book *You Can't Escape Wearing Shackles'* the au-
thoress shows her strong affinity with Swedenborg, whose mysti-
cism seems to match her female psyche. It is also perfectly clear
that her view of the human condition is not existentialist but
structuralist, lèvi-straussian and dialectically marxist—in
other words, far from simple. She sees our existence as a cycle or

a swing where we are integrated into a higher biological order on our insecure pilgrimage from orthoceratite to moon-invader. The only discordant notes in her harmonious and wise reflections, culled from Y and Z, are the personal sectors of the book that she might as well have refrained from writing."

The day for the oral had arrived. Spring was in full swing and it was a miracle that I had found any time at all for studying. My examination fear had increased with each passing minute, but the certainty that Lasse and Paris were waiting reduced the importance of the exam. To be sure, I had promised my parents to achieve my object in two years, four semesters, but by now I had more important matters than prestige to strive for. And yet: it is easy to push neuroses, doubts and sick thoughts to the background as long as your emotional conditions are favorable. You firmly believe that now you are well-balanced and mature, you have left the past with its tormenting dissonances behind; you have stopped taking notice of demands for achievement and advancement in a sick society. You feel you are above all that and you see it in all its pitiful and misanthropic guise, but you can only succeed in whatever you aspire to as long as you feel loved and secure.

Months and years pass and one day you are confronted by a situation that you coped with easily a year or two earlier but which today sends you straight into a padded cell.

To be judged and assessed. What an exquisite terror. What a hellish torment.

Once, when preparing for an oral in literature at the University, I almost went out of my mind. By that time I had started writing reviews for *BLM* and *Stockholms-Tidningen*. The professor knew that I was capable, I had written my alternative dissertation in the subject. More often than not, I preferred to read all of the set book rather than part of it, at least if the author had stirred my interest. On this occasion I withdrew from the world, had a wonderful time reading the books and forgot all about exams in the firm conviction that all was well in hand. The exam came closer and closer. The eventual outcome didn't matter all that much to me but it mattered that much more to Papa, and the pressure kept mounting. He had, after all, been willing to vouch for me and my academic career and he was growing older and more anxious about my future. Being a writer wasn't going to earn me a living. My debts were enormous, my debts to humanity, that was what my upbringing had impressed on me, always to consider the wants and demands of others. Hell! All these years of misunderstanding, as if I had lived to no purpose on the wrong premises, living a made-up life, not even here and now.

The evil day was upon me. I had postponed my exam several times and the professor had each time tried to persuade me to go ahead. He obviously believed in me but what did he believe? That I would be able to show off my hard-earned knowledge? That I would remember all those names and dates and show myself in possession of just so much learning as he had been conditioned to expect from me? Who had manipulated us and who had manipulated Papa to manipulate me into a nervous breakdown? I couldn't sleep at all the night before. Toward dawn I saw a huge shape glide slowly through the door. A dark angel, a man with black wings carrying a bucket of tar and a brush. I crouched before him, submissively, with my head bent so that he could draw a black cross on my back, along the spine and across my shoulders. I was doomed, defiled, sentenced to death and damnation. I was destined to be the culprit.

I wasn't asleep but awake. "The Vision" disappeared, the angel had gone. I had lost contact with reality but had the strength to lift the telephone and call Papa. I told him everything, that I had failed him, that this was farewell forever, that I was condemned to death, that I wasn't going to get my degree. Papa understood, of course he had understood everything but why on earth was I making such a song and dance about it? The professor repeated again that he was fully prepared to pass me if only I would put in an appearance. He sounded rather scared and embarassed. Had I taken leave of my senses? Yes, I had.

That spring I flunked my oral. I was supposed to pass in eight subjects—barring German that I had managed to clear in advance—compared with the four subjects that normal pupils are supposed to pass. That is, normal students trying to pass a normal student examination.

At the start of the proceedings, everything went swimmingly. I secured high marks in several of the language subjects, the sun shone on Stockholm and I saw myself setting off for Paris in a new white cap. Latin next. I had nurtured a faint hope about the oral, although I knew that pupils who have flunked the written test have very little chance of passing the oral. Not even Ovid, who I knew by heart, stood me in good stead. I had steeled myself against failing the Latin but not R.E. Unpleasant rumours had been circulated about the devilish R.E. teacher in that unfamiliar school but I had refused to take the rumor seriously and anyway, I believed that victory was mine as I had several A minuses already in the bag. Not until I entered the classroom where the teacher, the stranger, was waiting, did I admit to fear.

I think that talk about "vibrations" has deteriorated into sloppy usage, it is too often a blanket term describing somebody of whom you disapprove generally and want to throw suspicion on: "He has bad vibes" has become a fashionable and much frequented expression.

This teacher had bad vibes, without a doubt, really terrible vibes. His bluish-white taut skull with its lank wisp of hair glued to the temples seemed to stick its tongue out at me as soon as I entered the room. The empty holes he had instead of eyes already had my measure before they had seen me. He was in full formal dress, he was the sum total of everything I feared most without knowing exactly *what* that was. To me he was the personification of Death.

There is a certain type of man, when I meet them they detest me instinctively and nowadays that feeling is mutual. I used to try very hard to be loved and accepted by everybody, without exception. Thank Heaven that's a thing of the past.

This type of man feels somehow challenged by my looks, my shyness and my fear—in combination with my efforts to be strong and hide these shortcomings. Maybe it was my way of dressing (at that time fairly discreet) and my makeup (also fairly discreet) or something else that gave a "dangerous" impression, constituting a challenge to those who had decided, once and for all, never to approach the female animal. My very person seemed to illustrate the fall from grace, Pigalle and houses of ill repute or, possibly, to direct their thoughts toward little girls who anxiously try to hide, the ones one has to strangle after the punishing act of rape.

The first time I tried to pass a driving test, I was told by my instructor that "you'll pass with flying colors as long as you don't come up against Mr X who looks like Frankenstein." Needless to say, it was Mr X and I flunked.

It has always been the same lifeless, stiff, gray, correct, humour-less, taut, well-soldered superego, robot type of man who has damaged me, but I am not saying that everybody who damaged me necessarily looked like that or vice versa. A gray correct suit can hide an interesting and lively mind, but among those who occupy official or "superego" positions I always tend to get involved with the robots. I have this futile wish to vanquish and change them, make them blossom or rip their trousers off to help them slip into something more comfortable, ruffle their hair or caress their bald pates, if only to hinder these human pine trees from flattening and crushing all leaves and plants, women and everything that's alive. I know that they're often helpless as regards their actions but society promotes this kind of lifelessness to the point of excluding other, positive attitudes. Many, above all many women, have been damaged in the confrontation and I know that the gray robots most certainly have damaged me.

He faced me and I knew that the game was lost. "Enumerate the judicial rules of Olaus Petri" he hissed out of a throat as dry as the leaves in a hymnbook. Never in my life have I felt such a burning desire for anything as to be able to reel off those rules and stuff them, one by one, up the asshole of that infamously spiteful and negative Ignatius of Loyola. I'm afraid that he would probably have liked the treatment.

That was his only question. He turned to the external examiners in triumph and said derisively that, in his opinion, it was pointless wasting time on ignorant, genetically primitive swamp-dwellers like me.

Spring had changed into autumn and winter was approaching. Lasse and I were still together. My second attempt at passing the oral was scheduled for December, this time in five subjects, at Östra Real.

Lasse had been saying for some time that nobody but philistines bother about student exams. Not to mention that nonsense with the white cap, here we were of one mind. And far be it from either of us to celebrate such a ridiculously bourgeois exam.

I had hidden, deep down in a cellar corner of my memory, how my three older siblings, with garlands of flowers almost heavy enough to break their necks, were brought home in extravagantly decorated haycarts behind ponies from Slottsskogen. I had also hidden the singing, the throng of friends and parties at home, lasting for days and reverberating through town. All that past glory, white caps, ponies and all, lay at the bottom of memory, feeling dreadfully philistine.

Lasse and I had only invited a few close friends. We lived just round the corner from Lasse's parents, who were coming, together with some writers and Pierre, who later that night got into a fight with his habitual tormentor, il mafioso, who pulled a knife on him. Bettan, at that time called Elisabeth, was there; she was to become my dearest friend. A grammar school teacher, almost twenty-five years my senior, who taught me to believe in life, human values and revolution and who was to save my life time and time again, probably without realizing it. She had two sons, a broken marriage, was wise and torn, with a beautiful and brave soul in a fragile body.

Lou was there, she had fought at my side in school and we had laughed a lot together. Fittingly, she had bought me a white paper party hat, for a lark.

The exam went very well, exceeding my expectations in history and philosophy. A short rotund history teacher, the author of the definitive textbook, was my examiner. He asked what grade I was aiming at and I answered, full of embarrassment, that I'd be grateful for a pass. I'd been cramming the last few weeks but my head was absolutely empty, in particular was every trace of social science obliterated and that was what he always concentrated on, they said. I'd been studying day and night, at all times except when I was hanging over the loo, sick to my stomach from sheer nerves and fright.

And then, on the day, the little man stands before me with a smile that chases away all my fear. I found answers to all his questions, he allowed me to argue, we *talked*. He jollied the interrogation along indirectly, asking about the reigning dates of monarchs as an amusing game and chuckled gleefully when he told macabre deails: "the spears went right through, you might say" about the rusty bars you find on suits of armour, but with a melancholy irony covering all warmongering folly in the world.

Our discussion went on for so long that the external examiners fell asleep and I secured an A. It had been dialogue rather than interrogation, good rather than bad expectations, openness instead of closed doors, keys instead of explosives, kindness instead of threats.

I had made it in two years and one extra term. I had reason to feel proud before my family. But were they proud of me? No sign of that at first; later they sent congratulatory telegrams. Maybe they hadn't dared to believe in my success. There was no reception committee at the school. I hadn't asked for or expected it.

The results were expected around three o'clock. After that I was supposed to do the shopping for the party and hurry home for the preparations. Not even Lasse came to meet me at school; he had other, more important things to do, busy with a poem, maybe.

I remember that it snowed in the afternoon, light flakes from a grey leaden sky. Relatives of the students were waiting in the assembly hall and the names of the successful candidates were called.

Axelsson—with an A, which meant that I was among the first. A friendly applause for me from a group of strangers who didn't know me or weren't aware that I was indifferent to this bourgeois spectacle, stood above all the nonsense with flowers. Maybe they were a bit puzzled about me, when I slipped out in the school-yard, completely alone with nobody to meet me among the brave little troupe, shivering in the cold and waiting with their bouquets of flowers . . . flowers . . .

All the others students wore their brand new white caps but I didn't and the waiting crowd probably thought that I had flunked, with my bare head soon covered with the white snow.

I felt very lonely out there, not knowing what I ought to do. Was I supposed to wait for the others? Or should I simply leave . . . Everybody seemed to have somebody there, so I could do nothing but withdraw, slowly, with a heavy feeling of loss instead of pride in my independent free attitude to all the hullabaloo. I couldn't stop the tears pouring down and I looked up into the sky, the gray sky wrapping itself in its dark shroud or maybe opening up to scatter more snow . . . to give me my white cap. The dark sky was a symbol of my eternal longing and now I could talk to my mother, feeling unforgivably abandoned like a lost child. Here I am. Please be proud of me, Mama! You can see me, can't you? You do watch over me still . . . ? Or am I really this alone in the world? Is this how it is? How it has to be? Can't I ever hope for anything else?

We have to make an effort. Shake off laziness, try to reach our fellow human beings. To open up about yourself is to approach others, it is the first political act of solidarity, of unity. You acknowledge what is of common interest and respect differences in outlook, you learn to identify with the other person, you stop building fences that separate you from others, fences created by hate, but work instead for the common cause.

We are generally too blind and scared to see that a kind of salvation waits for us on each street corner; instead we rush past, complaining all the while that the sights are too painful to watch. We could learn from the suffering how to cure it, but we choose to ignore it, closing our eyes to the starving instead of giving them bread.

Many of us believe: Leaving the prison, we can only expect more floggings; freedom involves danger. We tend to forget that life is light as well as darkness, not only the dark dungeons inside but the light of freedom outside.